# BUSINESS IS BUSINESS 2

## A NOVEL

## SILK WHITE

**Good 2 Go Publishing**

ISBN:

Published 2015 by Good2Go Publishing
7311 W. Glass Lane, Laveen, AZ 85339
www.good2gopublishing.com
Twitter @good2gobooks
G2G@good2gopublishing.com
Facebook.com/good2gopublishing
ThirdLane Marketing: Brian James
Brian@good2gopublishing.com

Cover Design: Davida Baldwin

Printed in the United States of America

# BOOKS BY THIS AUTHOR

*Business Is Business*

*Business Is Business 2*

*Married To Da Streets*

*Never Be The Same*

*Stranded*

*Tears of a Hustler*

*Tears of a Hustler 2*

*Tears of a Hustler 3*

*Tears of a Hustler 4*

*Tears of a Hustler 5*

*Tears of a Hustler 6*

*Teflon Queen*

*Teflon Queen 2*

*Teflon Queen 3*

*Teflon Queen 4*

*Time Is Money (An Anthony Stone Novel)*

*48 Hours to Die (An Anthony Stone Novel)*

## WEB SERIES
*The Hand I Was Dealt*
*Episodes 1-8 Now Available Free On You Tube*

# Acknowledgments

To all of you who are reading this, thank you for stepping inside the bookstore, stopping by the library, or downloading a copy of Business Is Business 2. I hope you have enjoyed this read from top to bottom. My goal is to get better and better with each story. I want to thank everyone for all their love and support. It is definitely appreciated! Now without further ado Ladies and Gentleman, I give you *Business Is Business 2.*

$iLK WHiTE

# BUSINESS IS BUSINESS 2

# DERRICK

# 1

Derrick lay on his hospital bed catching up on some much needed rest. Doctors told him that he would be fine and would be able to return home in a few days, but for now, he needed to rest. The pills that the nurses gave Derrick, helped him sleep, and made his pain temporarily go away.

Derrick was counting sheep when all of a sudden his eyes snapped open as he heard the sound of a machine gun being fired. He sat up and wiped his eyes thinking that maybe he had been dreaming but when he saw his bodyguard hop up from the chair that rested down by the foot of his bed and run out into the hallway with a gun in his hand, he realized that this was real. Derrick sat in his bed with a scared look on his face as the sound of multiple machine guns could be heard ringing out. Whoever had attempted to kill Derrick the first time was back to finish the job. Derrick winced as he reached over and snatched out all the tubes and wires that were all hooked up to machines. He slowly guided his legs off the bed and slowly eased his way over to the door. Derrick was moving as slow as a snail but at the moment that was as fast as his body allowed him to move. He snatched his room door open and saw dead bodies sprawled all throughout the hallway. Derrick quickly reached down and removed the gun from the cop who was guarding his door holster. The sound of the loud gunfire seemed to be getting louder and louder which meant whoever was coming for Derrick, was getting closer and closer. Derrick limped down the hall as fast as he could, when he heard the gunfire stop he knew he had ran out of time. "Shit!" He cursed as he heard the sound of several men in combat boots making their way down the hall at a fast pace. Derrick quickly entered the first room he saw on his left, placed his back to the wall, and aimed his gun at the door. If Derrick was going out, he promised himself that he wasn't going alone. Derrick's palms began to sweat as he heard the footsteps stop directly in front of the door of the room that he was in. "Come on motherfucker, open the door," he whispered to himself. "Open the door."

Derrick saw the knob move as the door eased open. Without thinking twice, he pulled the trigger.

Boom!

Derrick dropped the first gunman with a bullet to the throat, when the man hit the floor, Derrick eyes opened wide in shock when he saw the police officer uniform on the dead man. It was at that moment that, Derrick knew he had fucked up. He dropped the gun on the floor and threw his hands up in surrender as several cops rushed inside the room and handcuffed, Derrick.

# JIMMY

# 2

"Somebody is trying to take out our family one by one," Jimmy said as him and Mike sat in Mike's apartment. "First they tried to murder pop, then they murdered, Big foot and Stoney."

"I have my ear to the streets so I'm sure we'll find out who's behind this sooner than later," Mike took a sip from his beer.

"Whoever is trying to murder our family is probably who's behind our stash apartment building being robbed," Jimmy said with an angry look on his face. The thought of somebody stealing something from him pissed him off even further, not to mention all the money they were going to miss out on. "When I find out who's behind this and it's off with their head."

"We may have to slow things down a little bit," Mike said. "My department is really coming down on us they want Derrick to rot in a jail cell and they're willing to do whatever it takes to get him off the streets." He knew how dirty his department could get when they really wanted something; the last thing he wanted was for the entire family to have to go down from one mistake.

"You know we can't do that," Jimmy told him. "We slow down and we could lose our territory. We've worked too hard to get to where we are today to just slowdown over a little heat."

"We have to be smart about this," Mike said. "If this blows up in our face, the entire family is done."

Jimmy was about to comment when he heard his cell phone ring. "Yo, what up?" he answered.

"Hey, Jimmy, Mr. Goldberg here," the family lawyer said in a dry, worried tone. "A team of hit men just tried to murder your father in his hospital room."

"What? Is he..."

"No he's still alive," Mr. Goldberg answered. "Your father snuck out of his room and tried to defend himself and wound up shooting a police officer by accident. I may be able to get him off on self-defense, but the DA wants your father so bad that he may have to sit for a little while until I can get this all settled out."

"So where is Derrick now?" Jimmy asked.

"They have him in custody with no bail. They're charging him with murdering a police officer," Mr. Goldberg said. "I can get him off on self-defense but he may have to sit until the judge gives us a court date and it's no telling when that could be."

Mike couldn't hear what was going on but just from the look on Jimmy's face, he could tell that it was bad news. Lately it seemed like nothing could go good for the Mason family. It felt as if someone had put a curse on the family.

"Keep me posted," Jimmy ended the call, turned and looked over at Mike. "Derrick is locked up."

# JACK MASON

## 3

Jack Mason sat in the strip club nursing a drink while bobbing his head to the music that blasted from the speakers. He was in good spirits due to the fact of how much money he made over the past month. He was slowly but surely taking over Derrick's territory one block at a time and the payoff was lovely. While all the other men in the strip club were tossing bills all throughout the air, Jack had his eye on one chick in particular. When he made eye contact with the chick that he was looking for, he gave her a slight head nod signaling for her come over to where he sat.

Kat walked through the strip club as if she owned the place. Every man in the place would love to have a shot at her in the bedroom and she knew it. Kat stood at 5'8" and weighed 160 lbs. She was thick in all the right places. She was a redbone that wore a long weave with the front of her hairstyle cut into a bang that stopped just above her eyebrows. "Jack Mason, long time no see. I heard you got hit with a ten-year bid a couple of years ago."

"Can't believe everything you hear Kat," Jack smiled as he sipped his drink. "Besides you know can't no jail hold a nigga like me."

"I guess," Kat said in an uninterested tone. She had heard plenty of stories about how grimy Jack was, so when she got a call from him her antennas went up immediately. "So how can I help you?"

"I have a job for you," Jack began. "And it pays $50,000."

The large amount of money quickly grabbed Kat's attention. "What do I have to do for that?" she asked with a raised brow.

"Are you still in the disposal business?"

"I am for that price," Kat said quickly. "So who's the target?"

"Jimmy Mason."

"Isn't he your nephew?" Kat asked with a disgusted look on her face. She knew Jack was a grease ball, but *damn.*

"*Was* my nephew, but forget all that, you want to make this money or not?"

"Yeah, I'm in," Kat said with a thirsty look in her eyes. She had already spent the $50,000 in her head and couldn't wait to get her hands on the cash.

"Here," Jack slipped Kat an envelope on the low. "That's a $10,000 deposit. You'll get the rest when the job is done." He stuck out his hand. Kat thumbed through the cash then shook Jack's hand.

Jack exited the strip club and slid in the back seat of the Range Rover that sat curbside waiting for him.

"How'd it go back there?" Black asked from behind the wheel.

"Kat is in," Jack said with a head nod.

"Can she be trusted?"

"Kat has taken down some of the biggest and baddest players in this game," Jack told Black. "So Jimmy should be a piece of cake."

"So after Jimmy, who's next?" Black asked glancing at Jack through the rearview mirror.

"Mike," Jack said as he pulled out his cell phone and dialed Mike's number.

# ERIC

# 4

Eric, Pistol Pete, Jimmy, and Mike all sat at the Mason family mansion, having a drink. The family lawyer Mr. Goldberg told them he had a message from Derrick Mason that he had to deliver. As the trio waited the lawyer's arrival, their minds began to wonder.

"So I wonder what the message is." Jimmy said out loud.

Eric shrugged. "Hopefully it's good news about pop being released soon."

"Or maybe he's found a new connect on the inside and has a way for us to get some new product." Mike said. Whatever the message was it had to be something big for Derrick to have all of them at the house. When Mr. Goldberg walked through the front door everyone's eyes lit up in excitement.

"Alright don't waste our time, spit it out," Jimmy said. He was tired of sitting around in suspense.

"Okay," Mr. Goldberg began. "I just came back from talking to Derrick Mason for over two hours and he had a lot to say." Mr. Goldberg cleared his throat and poured himself a drink. "First and foremost he wanted you all to know that he's very proud of you all and he has no idea how long he may have to sit behind bars, but no matter how long he has to stay in there he wants you all to not worry and he assured me that he would be fine. In his absence, he's chosen one of you to take over for him. One of you will be the new leader and head of this family," Mr. Goldberg took a slow sip from his drink. "Eric your father has chosen you to lead this family in his absence."

"Who me?" Eric looked around with a confused look on his face. "Why would he pick me to lead the family?"

"You're who he picked." Mr. Goldberg shrugged with a dumbfounded look on his face.

"You can't be fucking serious!" Jimmy barked. "Pops has officially lost his fucking mind."

Mike turned and looked at Eric and extended his hand. "Congratulations."

"Thank you," Eric shook his hand. He still couldn't believe that his father has picked him over Jimmy to be the head of the family business. This was a huge promotion but Eric knew since he had been chosen that now he would really have to step up to the plate. "Well we are going to keep things how they are for now," he said. "Jimmy you are still in control of security and enforcement," he turned to

Mike. "Mike I'm going to need you to keep all of these nickel and dime hustlers off of our corners and give me the heads up before the heat comes down on us."

"And what exactly are you going to be doing?" Jimmy said with an attitude. He was furious that Eric had been picked over him to run the family business.

"I'm going to find us a new connect and get us some product," Eric said.

"Can't do that genius!" Jimmy snapped. "If Chico finds out that we have a new connect, he'll send a million troops down here to kill us all."

"Fuck, Chico!" Eric barked. "We don't need him or his product If we sit around and wait, we'll lose all of our territory and I'm not about to sit around and let that happen." He was the boss now and had to make the tough decisions and do what was best for the family.

"You're going to get us all killed!" Jimmy yelled as he stood to his feet and stormed out.

"Jimmy is right," Mike said. "We are not strong enough to go up against Chico."

"Chico doesn't decide if our family eats or starves." Eric said simply. "He doesn't call the shots in this house."

"I hear you," Mike said as he looked down at his cell phone and saw Jack's name flashing across the screen. "I'm out of here. I'll call you tomorrow," he said then made his exit.

Once everyone was gone, Eric walked around the empty mansion with a drink in his hand with Pistol Pete close on his heels.

"So what's the plan?" Pistol Pete asked.

"I need you to go out and recruit as many soldiers as you can just in case we do have to go to war. This could get real messy."

\*\*\*

Eric walked through his front door and saw Kelly standing in the kitchen barefoot in a t-shirt, leggings, with her hair pulled up in a bun standing over the stove.

"Hey baby, you hungry?" Kelly asked as she walked over and gave Eric a hug.

"I'm not your baby." He quickly corrected. Eric didn't want to open that door back up, but he had to admit that ever since he allowed Kelly back into the house, she had been like a brand new person. She now treated Eric like her husband and not a stranger. It was seeming like she had really learned her lesson and decided to turn over a new leaf.

"Sorry Eric," Kelly apologized. "How was your day?"

"Eventful," Eric walked in the kitchen and poured him a shot of tequila. "My father chose me to run the family business in his absence."

"Are you serious?" Kelly couldn't believe her ears. "Why did he pick you?"

"I have no idea," Eric replied honestly. But he knew if Derrick chose him it was for a reason and he refused to let him down. "Pack your things we have to move into the mansion."

"Tonight?"

"No right now." Eric told her. He walked over to his floor to ceiling window and just stared out into the night. Eric knew he had to huge shoes to fill and was up for the challenge.

# MIKE

## 5

Mike pulled over on a block that belonged to the Mason family and killed the engine. He had gotten a call from Jack asking him to meet him there. Mike looked around and noticed that Jack was nowhere in sight. Mike didn't trust Jack one bit, but decided to come out and see what he had to talk about. He always believed in keeping his enemies close. Ten minutes later, Mike noticed a shiny black Benz pull up on the side of him. Mike had to take a double look when he saw Jack step out the Benz dressed in a tailored cream suit with a red tie.

Mike stepped out of his car to greet the man that acted as an uncle to him for so many years. "I didn't recognize you at first," Mike nodded towards the new Benz and expensive suit.

"I decided I should treat myself instead of cheat myself," Jack laughed. Mike laughed but took notice and silently wondered where he got the money to afford such expensive things being as though he hadn't been released from prison not too long ago.

"What's good though?" Mike asked.

"I had rolled through here the other day and saw some young knuckleheads on one of y'all's corners so I called you down here so you could see for yourself and make sure I wasn't bugging." Jack said as he led Mike down the block. "I was thinking maybe you could arrest them."

Mike chuckled. "I thank you for calling me, but Jimmy is the enforcer so I'll give him a call."

"But at least you can come and see what I'm talking about," Jack prodded. All he needed was to get Mike on the block and the rest would take care of itself. "Shit only gon take a minute."

Going against his better judgement, Mike decided to walk to the block with Jack. As the two walked, Mike saw a black van pull up to a screeching stop he noticed Jack duck down before the first shot rang out. Three bullets then ripped through Mike's chest taking him off his feet. The gunmen fired off twenty to thirty more shots before the gunfire came to an end.

Jack quickly picked himself up off the ground and hopped in the van while one of the gunmen hopped out the van and jogged back to his Benz, hopped inside and peeled off.

Mike laid sprawled out on the concrete leaking. He was thankful that he always wore his Kevlar vest. The bullets that hit his chest didn't penetrate through the vest but he did take a bullet to the thigh as well as his arm. Mike rolled over to his side, grabbed his cell phone, and called for an ambulance. Then he texted, Eric before everything went black.

# JIMMY

# 6

Jimmy stepped foot in the nightclub with three of his most trusted henchmen on his heels. The club's promoter immediately escorted Jimmy and his crew over towards his awaited VIP section. Jimmy needed to get out of the house and get some fresh air. He still couldn't believe that Derrick had put Eric in charge of running the family business. All the work that Jimmy had put in over the years for the family business had him feeling like some type of way about not being chosen. He sat on the couch as four bartenders brought bottles with sparkles spraying from the top over to his section. Jimmy grabbed a bottle of Cîroc and turned it up to his lips. His new driver slash bodyguard a longtime friend that went by the name Murder, stood behind him looking over the crowd for any signs of trouble.

Jimmy sat, bobbing his head to the Reggae beat that blasted from the speakers when he felt Murder tap him on the shoulder. "Damn look at shorty right there, she got the wagon!" Murder said nodding towards the woman in the spandex skirt with the huge horse ass.

"Damn shorty thicker than a bowl of oatmeal," Jimmy took another swig from his bottle as he eyed the chick closely she looked familiar as if he had saw her around somewhere before but he couldn't quite place his finger on it. "Go grab shorty up for me," Jimmy ordered.

\*\*\*

Kat stood on the dance floor, sipping on her drink, and doing a simple two-step. She hoped and prayed that her outfit was enough to grab Jimmy and his crew's attention. Kat sipped her drink when she felt a strong hand tap her on the shoulder. She turned and saw a man in an expensive suit standing before her, "Can I help you?"

"My boss would like to have a word with you," Murder told her.

Kat gave Murder a stank look, "Who's your boss?"

"Jimmy Mason," Murder nodded over to where Jimmy sat.

"Well, tell your *boss*," Kat emphasized on the word boss. "That I'm a grown ass woman and if he wants to talk to me then he better approach me the proper way," she turned and sipped her drink.

"Stop being difficult Ma," Murder huffed. He got ready to say another word but stopped when he realized that shorty wasn't budging. Murder walked back over to the VIP section and leaned down so that Jimmy could hear him. "Shorty want you to go over there and holla at her yourself."

Jimmy smiled. "Oh she one of those." He stood to his feet and removed his suit jacket, grabbed his bottle and headed down towards the dance floor. Jimmy approached the chick, stood in front of her, and sized her up.

"Nice of you to come down and talk to me like a real man," Kat said with a smile.

"Why you make me come all the way down here?" Jimmy smiled as he extended his arm and refilled Kat's glass. "Why you gotta be so difficult?"

"I think I deserve to be approached like a woman and not some random hoe," Kat said.

"Jimmy," he extended his hand.

"Kat," she shook his hand and noticed the iced out chunky bracelet that rested on his wrist.

Jimmy grabbed Kat's hand and led her back over towards the VIP section where the two laughed, joked, and ran through an entire bottle of Cîroc in a two-hour period. "So where you from?"

"Atlanta," Kat lied. The truth was she had seen Jimmy around long before she accepted the job to kill him. She knew exactly who he was and what he was capable of.

"What brings you all the way from Atlanta all the way to New York?"

"Opportunity," Kat answered quickly. "It's a lot of money out here and I need some of it."

Jimmy nodded his head, reached over and grabbed another bottle of Cîroc, then grabbed, Kat's wrist and slowly guided her down onto her lap and refilled her glass. Jimmy eased his hand down and let it rest on Kat's ass while he spoke. "I think you should leave now."

"Why?" Kat asked with a smile on her face. "Afraid you can't handle all this?" She slapped her ass for extra emphasis.

Jimmy smiled. "I've been known to ruin chick's lives, so I'm trying to give you the chance to leave now."

Kat leaned in and kissed Jimmy on the cheek. "I think I'll take my chances."

Jimmy got ready to respond when he saw a light scuffle break out by the entrance of his VIP section. Immediately, Murder and the rest of his team beat the man who was causing the disturbance half to death until security was finally able to get Jimmy's crew up off the man.

Once the brawl was over, Murder and the rest of Jimmy's crew escorted Jimmy and Kat out of the club. Jimmy stood outside checking out Kat's goodies when Murder pulled the SUV up to the curb and tapped the horn. Jimmy and Kat quickly slid in the back seat as the truck smoothly pulled away from the curb.

"So what you trying to get into?" Jimmy took a swig from his bottle as he openly checked Kat out.

"Shit, I'm with whatever," Kat replied kicking off her heels. The expensive shoes she wore were killing her feet and Kat couldn't wait to take them off so her feet could breathe.

Jimmy took another swig from his bottle then unzipped his zipper and pulled out his manhood. "Let me see what that mouth is about."

Kat smiled, then removed her gum from her mouth and tossed it out the window. "You sure you can handle this mouth?"

Jimmy grabbed the back of Kat's head and guided it down in between his legs. He closed his eyes and threw his head back in ecstasy as he felt the warmth of Kat's mouth slowly gliding up and down on his pole.

"Damn!" Jimmy moaned as he sat back and watched Kat do her thing. The way she was working her mouth, Jimmy could tell that Kat wasn't new to this. Just as Jimmy was about to explode, Kat stopped abruptly.

"Ma what you doing?" Jimmy asked with a confused look on his face and a hard dick in his hand.

"I'll finish when we get to your house," Kat kicked her lips seductively.

"Yo, Murder drop us off at the nearest hotel." Jimmy ordered. He couldn't wait to get Kat behind closed door and tear her apart. If her mouth was that good, Jimmy could only imagine how great her box would be.

Murder pulled up in front of the first hotel he saw, and handed the keys to the valet worker standing out front as the trio entered the hotel. Murder returned from the counter and pulled Jimmy to side. "You sure you can trust this bitch?"

"I'mma smash, leave the bitch in the room, then we out." Jimmy told him. Murder laughed as the trio then boarded the elevator. Kat stepped off the elevator holding her heels in her hand she was eager to get inside the room and get this over with.

"I'll be out here if you need me," Murder posted up in the hallway with his arms folded across his chest.

Jimmy gave Murder dap. "I'll be out in fifteen minutes." He said as him and Kat disappeared inside the room.

\*\*\*

"Get over here!" Kat growled through clenched teeth as she forcefully pushed Jimmy down on the bed and removed all of his clothes. Kat placed a condom in her mouth, took Jimmy's love stick in her mouth, and rolled the condom on him with her teeth. Kat then quickly mounted Jimmy and slipped him inside of her.

Kat planted her hands down on Jimmy's chest as she bounced up and down on Jimmy's nice sized rod. "Aww... yes... it's so big... oh my god!" She moaned loudly as she enjoyed Jimmy. Jimmy reached out and spread Kat ass cheeks apart as he plunged himself even deeper into her guts until he exploded. "Arghh!" He groaned, breathing heavily. "Damn!" He looked up at Kat with a smile on his face.

"You are an animal," Kat smiled. "But don't think you off the hook that easy we just getting started."

"I need a second to recharge."

"You got one minute," Kat said as she slowly unclipped the knife from off the back of her bra strap and quietly snapped it open.

Jimmy opened his eyes and was about to lean forward so he could suck on Kat's titties when he saw something glittering in her hand. "Fuck is you doing?"

Kat aimed for Jimmy's throat, and then drove the knife down with force. Jimmy squirmed out of the way just in time as the knife jammed down into his shoulder.

"Shit!" Jimmy cursed as he violently tossed Kat off the bed onto the floor. Kat bounced up off the floor with the quickness of a cat with the knife still in her hand. Kat tried to jab the knife in Jimmy's chest but he quickly jumped back before the blade could connect. Kat went to try and slice Jimmy again. Jimmy weaved the knife strike and landed a clean left hook that sent Kat's head into the wall and caused her to drop the knife. Kat roared like an animal as she ran and charged Jimmy tackling him as the two bounced off the bed and crashed loudly down to the floor.

\*\*\*

Murder stood outside the room when he heard a loud noise, followed by growling and moaning, and groaning. "Damn, Jimmy in there killing that pussy." He smiled as he placed his ear to the door the thought of the two having wild sex turned him on.

\*\*\*

Jimmy made it back to his feet first and went to punch Kat in her face, but was caught off guard when Kat scooped his legs from up under him and slammed him on his head. Kat's strength caught him by surprise. Jimmy raised his leg and kicked Kat in her face forcing her head to snap back violently. Jimmy hopped back up to his feet and unloaded a series of punches to Kat's exposed face. Before she got a chance to recover, Jimmy grabbed his gun from out of his holster and aimed it at Kat's head. "Who sent you bitch?"

Kat looked at Jimmy with blood running from her nose. "Fuck you!"

Without warning, Jimmy turned and shot Kat in the leg.

"Arghhh!" Kat howled as she clutched her leg and watched the blood run through her fingers. Seconds later, Murder came busting inside the room with his gun already drawn.

"Fuck is going on in here?" Murder looked around then aimed his gun at Kat's head.

"Last time I'm going to ask you," Jimmy growled through clenched teeth. "Who sent you?"

"Jack!" Kat spat. "He made me an offer I couldn't refuse."

"Why does he want me dead?"

"I don't know something about some territory." Kat winced in pain. "I need to get to a hospital."

Jimmy fired four shots into Kat's chest before he and Murder exited the room. Jimmy stepped on the elevator with a mean look on his face. He couldn't believe all this time it had been, Jack Mason behind all the killings. The more he thought about it the more it pissed him off. "I need you to send the cleanup crew to clean that mess up back there." Jimmy ordered.

"What about, Jack?" Murder asked.

"I'll take care of, Jack." Jimmy said as the two men stepped off the elevator.

# MIKE

# 7

Mike laid on the hospital bed with a sour look on his face. He had been answering questions all morning and he was relieved when the last cop had left his room. Living a double life was really beginning to wear him down mentally as well as physically. Mike hadn't told anyone yet but he was secretly thinking about getting out of the family business. It was getting harder and harder to keep the authorities off of the Mason family's ass. Mike laid in the hospital bed starving when he heard a light knock at his door, then saw a petite, dark skin woman enter his room and shut the door behind her.

"Aww baby, are you okay?" The dark skin woman asked in a concerned tone.

"I'm good," Mike said with a confused look on his face. He had never saw this woman before in his life and here she was acting as if they had some type of history together. The dark skin chick walked around the room looking for any bugs or cameras that may have been hid in the room. Once she was sure that the room wasn't bugged she sat down at the foot of Mike's bed.

"Hey, I'm Sonya. Eric sent me." She began. "He said it was too risky for him to come up here and talk to you so he sent me instead." Sonya pulled out a pen and note pad, turned and faced Mike. "Okay start from the beginning."

"Tell Eric that Jack is the one trying to destroy our family so he can take over the business."

"Anything else?"

"If I had to guess, I would say that Jack has a large team behind him or someone powerful that's backing him up." Mike told her.

"Eric asked me to ask you if you think any of your fellow officers have any idea about your dealings or involvement with the Mason family."

"Not that I know of," Mike answered quickly. He had been doing his best to keep his dealings with the Mason family as discreet as possible. Sonya stood to her feet, smiled, and said to go see Eric as soon as you are released from here.

Mike nodded as he watched Sonya disappear out the front door.

# MILLIE

# 8

Millie sat on the bleachers in the yard watching a couple of the other female inmates playing softball. It wasn't much but she needed something to get her mind off of what was going on out in the streets. She had been hearing about all the drama that was going on and it bothered her that there was nothing she could do to help from the inside. All she could do was pray that her family was able to maintain for a few more months until she was released and let back out into society. As Millie sat back on the bleachers, she saw Ebony walking across the baseball field headed in her direction. Ebony was a big, rough looking chick with a nasty attitude and bad temper. Ebony had a few girls smuggling drugs in for her but she was forced to sit on them because of Millie. She hated the fact that Millie had most of the C.O.'s in her pocket and was allowed to basically do what she wanted, when she wanted, and move around as she pleased. But now that Millie only had a few months left, Ebony was beginning to poke her chest out. Millie had even heard that Ebony was talking greasy about her and her family, but she chose not to address or confront Ebony because she knew if she was involved in a violent act, it could cost her a few more months, maybe even years of her freedom and Millie was too smart to let a clown like Ebony outsmart her.

Ebony walked across the middle of the baseball field with no regard for the people who were playing. "That ball hit me and I'm fucking all you bitches up!" She shouted with an intense look on her face. Immediately the ball game came to a standstill until Ebony was across the field. Ebony walked up to the bleachers, looked at Millie, took one last drag from her cigarette, and then flicked it. "Bitch we need to talk."

"Ya'll ain't got nothing to talk about!" Pam spoke up. She was Millie best friend and very protective. She knew Ebony's intentions and refused to let her get Millie in trouble when she was so close to getting out.

"Bitch I wasn't talking to you!" Ebony counter never taking her eyes off of Millie.

"It's cool," Millie told Pam as she stood up and walked off to the side so her and Ebony could talk privately.

"How can I help you?"

"Listen!" Ebony began. "I think it's time that you start to share some of your real estate. I mean especially since you'll be going home in a few months."

"Once I'm gone you can do as you please," Millie said in a calm tone. She knew that Ebony couldn't wait until she was gone so she could flood the jail with her drugs, but unfortunately, for her Millie hadn't been released yet.

"Listen Millie, I'm coming to talk to you woman to woman," Ebony said, looking Millie dead in her eyes. "Shit gon have to change around here you've had control over this entire jail for years and I think it's fair that since you about to be going home soon that you allow me to get my little empire started now."

"I understand where you coming from," Millie told her. "But you can't expect me to stop my money now just because I'm about to go home, like I told you earlier once I'm gone you can do as you please it's nothing personal it's just business is business."

"Well you got three days to change your mind or this matter will become personal!" Ebony growled doing her best to try and intimidate Millie. "I've sat back and kept quiet long enough, either you going to let me eat or we gon have to bang out the choice is yours I'll be back to see you in 72 hours."

Millie shook her head as she watched Ebony walk off and blend in with the rest of the crowd in the yard. Millie knew when her time got short that all types of chicks would be coming out of the wood works gunning for her spot. She called Pam over with a head nod. "Get the team ready, we going to war in 72 hours."

# ERIC

# 9

Eric sat behind his desk in his office with a disturbed look on his face. He had just got word back that it was none other than Jack who had been trying to destroy the Mason family empire. The news didn't come to a surprise to Eric but it did piss him off. He knew that Jack was a snake, but he never expected him to go this far. Eric looked up at Pistol Pete. "I need you to grab some soldiers and make this problem go away."

"I'll take care of it," Pistol Pete said as he exited Eric's office. Eric sat behind his desk and ran his hand across his waves and let out a loud sigh he had no idea running the family business would be so much work. A soft knock at the door grabbed Eric's attention. "Come in."

Kelly stepped foot in the office and could immediately see the stress on Eric's face. "Hey baby I was just checking to make sure you were alright?"

"Yeah I'm good baby." Ever since Eric had allowed, Kelly to move back into the house, she had been acting like a brand new person, Eric could tell that she was truly sorry for what she had done and had learned her lesson. But with all that being said in the back of his mind it was still a part of him that still didn't trust her. "What's on your mind?"

"Was just a little worried about you," Kelly walked over and slid down on Eric's lap. "Ever since you've taken over the family business you've been stuck in this office stressed out and honestly I'm getting a little worried about you."

"Nothing to worry about," Eric said quickly. "I have everything under control."

"Any word on when Derrick's getting out of jail?" Kelly hoped and prayed that Derrick was released as soon as possible so that Eric could go back to living a normal life. She could tell that Eric was trying to be strong, but deep down inside this wasn't him.

"Mr. Goldberg said he should be hearing something any day now about my father getting out." Eric said as he moved Kelly off of his lap. "Go put on something nice I'm going to take you out to eat."

"Really?" Kelly's face lit up with excitement this would be the first time that the two went anywhere together since she was allowed back inside the house. "I'll be ready in an hour." Kelly said as she ran off to get dressed.

Eric sat behind his desk when he felt his cell phone vibrating in his pocket. "Yeah." He answered.

"This is, Chico," he spoke in a calm tone. "I'm calling to inform you that Joey Alvarez's body has been found and me as well as all the other members on the council agree that the Mason family is responsible for his death."

"How ya'll figure that?" Eric asked with a raised brow. "Just because ya'll found his body doesn't mean that we were responsible for Alvarez's death."

"Joey Alvarez was last seen entering your father's home," Chico pointed out. "Which tells me if your father didn't kill Joey Alvarez himself then he had it done or either he knows who did it."

"I hear what you saying Chico, but you have no hard evidence you basically just going off of your gut and I don't think that's fair." Eric said.

"Listen Eric this isn't the court of law it's the streets so I don't need no hard evidence and let me tell you one thing about my gut," Chico paused for a second. "My gut is always right and I always follow my gut."

"You're making a big mistake Chico, our family is innocent," Eric pleaded. He knew he was fucked, but right now, he was just trying to buy his family some time.

"A hit squad will be coming to kill you and everyone in your entire family within the next 24 hours please don't try to run or skip town because wherever you go I'll find you." Chico said in a calm tone.

"Chico, my father has brought you millions of dollars and this is how you repay him? There has got to be another way, another way to let us clear our name at least. I'm telling you me and my family is innocent." Eric told him.

"Listen Eric, I personally love your father and your entire family. I swear I do, but business is business." Chico said then hung the phone in Eric's ear.

"Shit!" Eric cursed loudly. He knew there was nowhere to run or hide, Chico's hit squad would hunt him and his family down like a pack of dogs until every last one of them was dead and gone.

The door to Eric's office swung open and his hand immediately went to his holster.

"Baby it's just me," Kelly said with her hands up and a frightened look on her face. "You okay?"

"Yeah I'm fine," Eric said as he stood up and buttoned the top button on his suit jacket. "What you all dressed up for?"

"You told me to get dressed so we could go to dinner," Kelly said with a confused look on her face.

"Sorry baby," Eric apologized. "Where do you want to go?"

"You sure you alright baby?"

"Stop asking me am I alright. I told you I'm fine." Eric snapped. "I'll be ready in five minutes." Eric quickly ran upstairs and removed his suit jacket and shirt he then walked over to his closet and pulled out a Kevlar vest and strapped it across his chest. He wasn't about to take no chances.

Eric made his way back downstairs and saw Pistol Pete snacking on a bag of chips. "I'm about to take Kelly to dinner. I need you and three other men to suit up and join me."

Instantly Pistol Pete could tell that something was wrong. "What's wrong?"

"Chico called and said they found Joey Alvarez's body," Eric shook his head. "Said me and the entire family is dead."

"Damn!" Pistol Pete spat. "That's bullshit!"

"Yeah I know but it is what it is," Eric shrugged.

"So what's the plan?"

Eric smiled. "Ain't no plan. When they come, we banging out."

"I'll round up as many soldiers as I can," Pistol Pete said. There were already twelve armed bodyguards posted up out front of the mansion and Pistol Pete along with two other guards inside watching over Eric. "Oh and by the way I sent a few soldiers out to take care of Jack."

Eric nodded. "Good job and make sure you get word to Jimmy and Mike. Tell them it's time to go to war."

# JACK

# 10

Jack sat in the passenger seat of the new sleek black Benz staring out the window. He couldn't believe how fast his life was changing right before his eyes. Less than a month ago, he was a nobody and now here he was riding around in a brand new Benz, wearing thousand dollar suits. Jack loved his new life and was willing to do anything to keep it. Behind the wheel, Black drove as the sounds of Young Jeezy bumped through the speakers. "What you over there thinking about?"

"I just got word that Chico is sending a hit squad to take out the Mason family. That means the streets are officially ours now," Jack said with a crooked smile on his face. "All they had to do was play nice but no they wanted to be greedy." He said under his breath. Most of his life, Jack Mason got looked over and was forced to play the background, but not anymore. From now on people were not only going to respect him but fear him as well. "Yo, pull over right here!" Jack barked when he spotted one of the Mason family employers standing on one of his corners.

The passenger side door swung open and Jack stepped out the vehicle and headed straight for the man standing on the corner followed by Black.

"You got permission to be standing on this block?" Jack asked looking down at the shorter man.

"Who the fuck is you?" The man spat with his face crumbled up. "I work for the Mason family."

"Check this out my man," Jack began. "This block is now under new management. If I catch you on this block again it's going to be fireworks."

"Fireworks?" The man echoed taking an aggressive stance. "Don't threaten me with a good time." He said as his hand slipped down towards his waistline. Before the man could grab his gun from off his waist, Jack caught him with a sucker punch and grabbed his wrist denying him access to his weapon. While Jack and the man scuffled, Black crept up behind the man and swept his legs from up under him. The man's gun fell from his waist and hit the ground with a loud clank.

"You crazy!" Jack barked as him and Black stomped the man's face into the concrete. Jack pulled his 9mm from his holster. He thought about shooting the man but changed his mind when he saw the crowd that had formed out of nowhere. Jack raised his leg and stomped the man's face into the concrete one last time before him and Black returned back to their vehicle.

Just as Black pulled away from the curb, Jack saw an old school car pull up with two men hanging out of the window. He immediately recognized one of the men as Jimmy Mason. Jack quickly ducked his head down as bullets tore through the passenger door and windows. The loud sound of tires screeching filled the air as Black recklessly pulled out into traffic. Black stepped on the gas flying right through a red light as bullets pinged loudly off the body of the car.

Jack felt the car swerve, looked up, and saw Black with his head resting on the steering wheel. "Shit," he cursed as he held on for dear life as the car ran off the side of the road off into the woods. The car ran over bushes and hit hard bumps until finally crashing into a tree.

\*\*\*

Jimmy and, Murder hopped out the van and headed down into the woods. They slowly made their way down the steep hill towards the mangled vehicle. Jimmy was planning to put an end to Jack and his grimy ways once and for all. Jimmy slowly crept around to the front of the car and snatched the door open only to find the passenger seat empty.

"Fuck!" Jimmy barked as he looked around and saw no sign of Jack.

# MIKE

# 11

Mike stepped onto the hospital elevator and breathed a sigh of relief. It had been two long weeks and they were now finally releasing him from the hospital. When he turned his phone back on, it was blowing up with missed calls and messages. Mike clicked two unread messages from Eric. His mood immediately changed from good to sour after reading Eric's text message about Chico putting a hit on the entire family. No matter what happened it seemed like things kept getting worse and never better. Mike stepped off the elevator and immediately noticed two Columbian-looking men with no nonsense looks on their face pretending to be reading an old newspaper. The jeans and trench coats were a dead giveaways, especially with it being the middle of summer. Mike walked towards the exit and just as he suspected the two Columbian men got up and headed towards the exit as well. Mike discreetly pulled his 9mm from his holster and cocked a round into the chamber. He'd just got out of the hospital and wasn't about to go back. Mike thought about turning around and opening fire on the two men but then thought about all the innocent people, he would put in harm's way if he did that, so he decided to lead the two men out into the parking lot and hold court there.

Mike walked through the parking lot and as soon as he was about to confront the two men a fellow officer walked up on him.

"Detective Brown its good to see you back on the streets." The officer said with a smile. His smile quickly faded when he noticed the gun that Mike held in his hand. "Is everything alright?"

"I think these men are following me," Mike said in a light whisper. The officer looked over Mike's shoulder and saw the two men in trench coats.

"Is there something I can help you gentlemen with?" The officer asked in a stern tone. Before Mike could fully turn around, the officer's head exploded like a melon as blood splattered all over Mike's face. Mike quickly fired two shots over his shoulder blindly as he took cover behind the closest car in the parking lot. He heard one of the gunmen drop to the ground as several bullets pinged loudly against the body of the car.

When the taller gunman saw his partner hit the floor, he went crazy. He pressed his finger down on the trigger and lit the car up.

Mike moved around to the other side of the vehicle in a low crouch when he got a clean shot of the gunman he took the shot.

Blocka!

Mike watched as the second gunman crumbled down to the ground with a gunshot wound in his neck. He slowly walked up on the gunman and kicked his gun out of arms reach. "Who sent you?"

The gunman flashed a bloody smile. "There are thousands of us in the states. It won't be long until you and your entire family are dead." He said as he took his last breath.

Mike stood over the dead man and shook his head. It was obvious these gunmen had no respect for human life if they were willing to have a shootout in a crowded hospital with a cop. Mike knew this was going to be an ugly outcome. He just hoped and prayed that his family was on the winning side.

# JIMMY

# 12

"Look at the flicka da wrist!" Jimmy sang along with the rest of the club as he watched the dancefloor go crazy. He got word that the Columbians were in town and looking to kill anyone with the last name Mason. The last thing he was going to do was sitting around and cry. The Mason family had made their bed now it was time for them to sleep in it. Jimmy  stood in the VIP section of the club surrounded by thirty of his best goons. A Kevlar vest protected his chest, not to mention him and his crew were armed to the tee. All Jimmy knew was violence so this wasn't nothing new to him, but what did bother him was the amount of Columbians shooters that were said to be in America just for the Mason family. Word on the streets was that five thousand Columbian hit men were sent to take out the, Mason family.

Sitting on the couch behind Jimmy was his new girlfriend Cherokee. She was a caramel complexion with full lips and the body of a stripper. She rocked a short cute hairdo. In her hand was a glass of wine. Cherokee stood up and tapped Jimmy on his shoulder. "Can I talk to you for a second?" She said leading him over in the corner.

"What's up?"

"Don't you think you should slow down," Cherokee nodded down at the bottle that Jimmy held in his hand. "Just in case these punk-ass Columbians show up you need to be on point." She pointed out. Cherokee new all about the Columbian hit and still chose to deal with Jimmy even though she knew being with him could eventually cost her, her life.

Jimmy flashed a drunken smile and palmed Cherokee's ass. "You talking like you love me or something."

Cherokee plunked the bottle from Jimmy's hand. "I do."

"Let me holla at you for minute," Murder cut in and pulled Jimmy over to the side. "Just got a text from one the look outs outside he said that four pickup trucks just pulled up outside with a bunch of Columbians men carrying assault rifles!"

"Right now?" Jimmy asked. As soon as the words left his mouth the sound of gunfire crackled through the air. Jimmy quickly ran over towards the couch, removed a tech-9 from under the cushion, and let it rip. Partygoers ran for their lives stepping over one another in an attempt to get to the exit.

Jimmy put down the twelve Columbian men that stormed inside the club. "Yeah motherfuckers!"

He yelled with a smile. Seconds later, the smile was quickly removed from his face when he saw sixty Columbians run up in the club shooting anything moving as if it was the Wild West.

"Come on motherfuckers!" Jimmy yelled as he and his crew returned fire on the Columbians.

Cherokee stood crouched behind the sofa as she watched several bodies drop right next to her. She reached out and picked up one of the dead goons 9mm. She looked up and saw a Columbian man with wild hair trying to creep up on Jimmy from behind. Cherokee quickly snuck up on the Columbian and blew his brains out. Jimmy spun around and saw Cherokee standing there holding a smoking gun in her hand.

"Come on baby we have to go!" Jimmy yelled as he grabbed, Cherokee by the arm and roughly escorted her towards the back exit. Jimmy and Cherokee spilled out of a side door and jetted down the hall when they saw two Columbian men bust through the emergency staircase. Jimmy quickly raised his arm and put both gunmen down.

Blocka! Blocka!

Jimmy and Cherokee stepped over the two dead bodies and quickly ran down the stairs when they reached the main floor. Jimmy slowly opened the side door and peeked out before two shots loudly bounced off the metal door inches away from his head. "Shit!" Jimmy cursed as he slammed the door as several more shots exploded into the door. Jimmy quickly removed his suit jacket and tossed it down to the floor. "You know how to use that thing?" He said looking down at the gun in Cherokee's hand. She nodded her head with a scared look on her face.

"Good cause on the count of three I'm going to open this door and air these Columbian motherfuckers out!" Jimmy paused for a second to take in Cherokee's reaction. "While I do that I want you to run to the car and wait for me at that hotel that I took you too when we first met."

"But what about you?"

"Don't worry about me, I'll be fine." Jimmy kissed Cherokee on the lips. "One... Two... Three!" Jimmy pushed the door open and blindly opened fire on the Columbians keeping his body In front of the metal door using it as a shield. Cherokee kicked her heels off and dashed from out of the building she ran full speed. As she ran, she felt bullets whizzing by her head and face. Cherokee made it to the Benz, hopped in, and pulled out of the parking lot like a mad man.

Jimmy fired round after round until his gun clicked empty. He peeked around the corner and saw several Columbian men closing in on him. "Shit!" Jimmy cursed as he ran and dived behind a rusty looking dumpster. With no more bullets, there wasn't much he could do but wait to die. The loud pinging of bullets ricocheting off of the dumpster caused Jimmy's stomach to leap up into his throat. All he could hear was the sound of footsteps getting closer and closer. Jimmy closed his eyes and prepared to die.

"A nigga!" He heard a voice shout. Jimmy opened his eyes, looked up, and saw, Murder standing over him holding a smoking gun in his hand. "Come on we gotta go!" He yelled as he helped, Jimmy up to his feet. The two men quickly ran through the parking lot, hopped in one of gunmen's pickup trucks, and peeled out.

# MILLIE

# 13

Millie stepped out of her cell and was escorted straight towards the visiting room. They had been calling her name over the loud speaker but she didn't hear it because she was sleeping. Millie stepped foot in the visiting room and smiled when she saw Eric sitting at the table waiting for her. "Hey son it's good to see you!" She smiled as she wrapped him in a bear hug. "So how have you been?"

"Hanging in there," Eric said in a voice just above a whisper.

"Talk to me, what's been going on?"

"Chico put a hit out on the entire family,"

"What!" Millie snapped. "When the fuck was someone planning on telling me?"

"Didn't want to worry you while you were in here," Eric explained. "They found Alvarez's body."

Millie shook her head. "I'll make some calls and see if I can fix this somehow."

"I can handle it mom."

"How?"

"Simple," Eric said with a straight face. "We going to war!"

Millie gave Eric a sad look. "I never wanted this life for you." She paused for a second. "I fought so hard to keep you away from this."

"I know ma, but I'm grown and make my own decisions," he told her. He knew him sitting across this table right now was breaking his mother's heart, but he had been chosen to run the family business while Derrick was away. "How have you been holding up in here?"

"I'll be home in 90 days but you know what they say, these last days be the hardest." Millie flashed a phony smile. She hoped and prayed that when she made it home her family would still be alive. "You be safe and stay alive."

Eric smiled. "I'll be waiting outside to pick you up in 90 days."

"I'm going to hold you to that," Millie said as she hugged Eric tightly then headed back to the search room. While all the other female inmates were being searched, Millie stood off to the side and had a conversation with one of the correction officers she had on her payroll. Thirty minutes later, Millie stepped foot back on the tear and could immediately feel the tension in the air. Millie walked towards her cell where she saw her best friend Pam waiting for her. Millie walked up and bumped fist with, Pam. "What's the word?"

"Ebony and a few of her home girls are waiting for you in the shower." Pam told her.

"Right now?" Millie asked. She knew that she and Ebony were going to end up going head up sooner or later. Ebony was jealous of Millie and wanted to be her. Millie stepped in her cell and removed her shirt while Pam taped several magazines and paperback books around Millie's organs. Millie reached under her mattress and removed her shank, then walked over to her sink, opened a jar of Vaseline and greased her face up. She was no stranger to combat and had been waiting to put Ebony in her place for a while now.

"Come here," Pam said as she pulled Millie's hair into a bun.

Millie stepped out her cell and headed straight for the showers. On the walk to the showers, several of the females that worked for Millie got up and followed her into the showers. Millie stepped in the showers and saw Ebony standing there with several of her home girls behind her.

"How you wanna do this?" Millie asked in a calm tone.

Ebony looked down and saw the shank glistening in Millie's hand. "You tell me," she began. "All I'm asking is that you allow me to open up shop since you about to leave."

"I already told you, you can do as you please once I leave." Millie told her.

"Well that ain't gon work," Ebony spat as one of her home girls handed her a knife. Ebony moved in blur as she tried to catch Millie off guard. She tried to jab Millie in her chest with the blade but Millie was quick on her feet and quickly danced out of reach and caught Ebony with a counter left hook to the chin. Millie charged in and jammed her shank in the pit of Ebony's stomach but luckily for her she had several books and magazines wrapped around her body. Ebony swung her knife and sliced Millie's arm, causing her to drop her shank. When Ebony saw opportunity, she took advantage she rushed Millie and forced her back up on the sink. Ebony tried to stab Millie in her face, but Millie grabbed Ebony's wrist right before the blade could pierce through her eye. Millie twisted Ebony's wrist backwards until the knife fell from her hand she then followed up with a head butt.

Pam and the rest of, Millie's crew stood on the sideline watching the two women go at it when she noticed a few of Ebony's home girls inching closer and closer towards the action. "Back up!" Pam yelled to Ebony's crew.

"Bitch you back up!" The heavyset dark skin chick countered as she balled up her fist. Pam and the dark skin chick exchanged a few more words before an all-out brawl broke out in the shower room. Minutes later, several correction officers stormed inside the shower room and saw what looked like a royal rumble taking place right before their eyes. Millie rolled on top of Ebony and unloaded several hard punches to her face before two CO's tackled her from off top of, Ebony.

# ERIC

# 14

"Baby why don't you come to bed?" Kelly said with a worried look on her face. She had watched Eric pace back and forth for the past two hours and every five minutes she would notice him look out the window.

"I'll come to bed in a minute baby," Eric said as he stared out the window. He didn't know what it was but something in his gut was telling him that something bad was going to happen tonight.

"Is everything alright?"

"Yeah everything is fine," Eric lied.

"Baby don't lie to me," Kelly crawled out of bed and joined Eric at the window. She pressed her naked body up against his back. "If something is going on I should know about it,"

"Everything is fine," Eric continued to lie. The last thing he wanted to do was upset or scare Kelly.

Kelly place her hands on her hips. "So you just going to lie to me right in my face?" She asked. "I know something is wrong because your gun closet is unlocked."

"Some really important people put a hit out on our family." Eric finally told her.

"So that explains all the extra security," Kelly sat on the edge of the bed. She knew that the outcome was going to be bad but the question was how bad.

"If you want to leave I understand." Eric said. "Where ever you want to go I'll pay for it."

Kelly stood up, grabbed Eric's face with both hands, and looked him in his eyes. "I already lost you once and I swear until I die I'll stand by your side." She said then kissed him on the lips. She had no clue how much hearing that meant to Eric.

"Thanks baby I just want..." Eric's words got caught in his throat as the sound of gunfire crackled through the air. Eric quickly walked over to the window and looked out. His eyes widened in fear as he saw what looked to be an army of men climbing over the iron gate and onto his property. Eric quickly pulled out his phone and dialed Jimmy's number. "They coming for me they're at my house now!"

"Say no more. I'm on my way!" Jimmy ended the call.

Eric ran to the closet, grabbed a silk robe, and tossed it at Kelly. "Here put that on!" He then walked over to the gun closet and handed her a Mac-10.

Kelly looked down at the machine gun in her hand. "I don't know how to use this."

"You gon learn today!" Eric said as he strapped on a Kevlar vest, grabbed two 9 mm, and stuck them down into his waistband. He then grabbed the AR-15 from off of the top shelf and walked over to the window. Eric aimed the rifle at the Columbian hit squad and began picking them off one by one. It seemed like the more Columbians he shot, the more that appeared. Eric took a second to reload his weapon when several bullets rain in through the window he quickly ducked down as a series of bullets peppered the wall leaving holes the size of a golf ball. Eric sprung back up to his feet and squeezed down on the trigger. He swayed his arms back and forth taking out as many of the Columbian shooters as possible. Eric ducked down again so he could reload his weapon again when out of nowhere a grenade flew through his window landing right next to him. "Shit!" He cursed loudly as he quickly hopped to his feet, grabbed Kelly, and headed for the door. The couple only made it a few steps before a loud explosion erupted and the force tossed them through the air like a rag doll, sending their bodies violently crashing through the wall as if it was made out of wet tissue.

Eric sat up and looked around for his rifle but it was nowhere in sight. He had lost consciousness for a few seconds but he had no clue how long he had been out for. Eric peeled himself off the ground then reached down and slapped Kelly's cheek a few times trying to get her to come back around but it was no use, she was out of it. Eric placed two fingers up against Kelly's neck and breathed a sigh of relief when he felt a pulse. His body jumped as he heard a loud roar of gunfire erupt. The gunshots were so loud that Eric could instantly tell that the Columbian gunmen had now made their way into the mansion.

"Urggh!" Eric growled as he lifted Kelly up and tossed her body over his shoulder. From the sound of the gunshots, Eric could tell that he was running out of time. He removed one of the 9mm's from his waistband as he carried Kelly towards the panic room. Eric made it a few feet down the hall when one of the doors opened and a Columbian man barged out. Eric and the gunman both fired off several shots simultaneously, two bullets exploded in the mid-section of Eric's vest sending him stumbling back into the wall while his two shots hit the gunman in his chest and neck dropping him instantly. Eric walked up on the wounded gunman and shot him point blank range in the face.

Blocka!

Eric's entire body was in pain it felt like he had just been in a bad car accident, but he couldn't let that stop him he had to get Kelly to the panic room. He struggled down the hall when another

Columbian gunman spun around the corner; Eric quickly put the gunman down with two shots to the stomach.

Blocka! Blocka!

Eric reached the panic room and quickly punched in the codes and pushed his way inside the safety room. He gently laid Kelly down on the floor then exited the panic room and slammed the door shut behind him. When Eric looked up he almost shit in his pants when he saw a Columbian man aiming a rifle at his face. Eric closed his eyes and prepared for what was going to come next. A loud blast erupted and Eric opened his eyes and saw the Columbian man laid out on the floor with a bullet hole in the back of his head, standing behind the dead Columbian stood Pistol Pete holding a smoking gun. "Happy to see me?"

Eric flashed a thankful smile. "Thank you."

"There's about thirty to forty Columbians downstairs," Pistol Pete said as he picked up the dead Columbian's rifle from off the floor. Eric picked up an A.K. 47 from off the floor as the sound of several machine guns being fired all at the same time sounded off.

"Sounds like the 4th of July down there," Pistol Pete joked. "You ready?"

Eric nodded his head as he followed, Pistol Pete downstairs right into the heart of the gunfight.

Eric ran through the living room with his finger pressed down on the trigger. Rat, Tat, Tat, Tat! He put down several gunmen as bullets whizzed by his head. Eric stood in a low hunch behind the counter on a silent count of three he sprang from behind the counter and opened fire on anything moving. It seemed like every time a Columbian went down; four more appeared out of nowhere. Eric saw a Columbian creeping up on Pistol Pete from behind; he quickly aimed his rifle at the gunman and squeezed the trigger only to hear. Click!

"Shit!" Eric cursed as he grabbed a knife from out of the knife block. Just as the gunman was about to line Pistol Pete up, Eric jabbed the knife in the gunman's back all the way to the handle then gave it a strong twist. Eric thought about jamming the knife in the gunman's back again until he heard several footsteps coming from behind him. Eric spun just as more gunfire filled the air. He used the gunman as a human shield as bullets riddled and rocked the gunman's body. Eric back peddled until his back hit the wall. There was nowhere left for him to run and standing in front of Eric stood four gunman. Out the corner of his eye, Eric saw a figure dressed in all black enter through the kitchen window with the quicken and quietness of a cat.

The man dressed in all black quickly fired four silenced shots. Pst! Pst! Pst! Pst! dropping all four of the remaining gunmen. When the gunman removed his black hood, Eric smiled when he saw that the man in all black was none other than Jimmy.

"You scared the shit out of me," Eric said holding his heart.

"We good. I have a few of my men outside taking care of the rest of the trash," Jimmy said with a smile. "But fuck all that, we need to find a place where we can lay low from Chico's army as well as the cops."

"I'll figure something out," Eric said as he turned towards Pistol Pete. "Get Mr. Goldberg on the phone." Just as Pistol Pete pulled out his phone. The window on the other side of the kitchen exploded as a cocktail bomb landed on the kitchen floor, followed by two more than three more. Within seconds, the entire kitchen was on fire. Jimmy, Eric, and Pistol Pete quickly rushed towards the nearest exit.

"Shit, Kelly's still in the house!" Eric yelled.

"I can't let you go back in there," Jimmy said as he grabbed, Eric. Eric quickly broke free of his brother's grip and ran back inside the burning house. The house was so smoky that Eric could barely see anything he had to use his instincts and memory until he reached the panic room. The smoke badly assaulted his eyes and nose as he punched in the code. Once inside the panic room, Eric quickly scooped Kelly up and tossed her body over his shoulder like a fireman.

"What's going on?" Kelly couched repeatedly. She tried to look around but had no luck the thick black smoke made it hard for her to do anything.

Jimmy and Pistol Pete stood outside watching the mansion burn when out of nowhere they saw Eric come running out the front door with his pant legs on fire. They quickly rushed and put out the fire on his legs.

"Come on we have to go!" Jimmy said as the sound of several sirens filled the air.

# PISTOL PETE

# 15

Pistol Pete sat behind the wheel cruising through the city while Eric sat in the backseat staring blankly out the window. He knew that Eric had a lot on his plate being the man in charge. Now that Eric was the boss, Pistol Pete knew there would be a lot of people gunning for him and it was his job to keep Eric safe. He had promised Millie that he would protect Eric with his life and that's just what he planned on doing. Pistol Pete pulled into the warehouse and immediately saw Jimmy, Mike, and the rest of the crew standing around. In the center of the warehouse, sat a man tied down to a chair. Pistol Pete placed the gear in park as him and Eric stepped out.

Eric stepped out the truck with an aggravated look on his face. "Who the fuck is this guy?"

"This the motherfucker right here that gave those Columbian fucks the code to your front gate," Jimmy said as he slapped the man in the back of the head.

Eric looked down and realized that the man tied down to the chair was none other than one of the security guard's he had hired to guard the property. Eric pulled his 9mm from his waistband.

"Please don't do this. They told me if I didn't give up the code they were going to kill my whole family!" The former security guard said in a frantic tone. "I swear to god you know I would never..."

Blocka!

Eric watched as the man's brains popped out the back of his skull, then holstered his gun as if nothing had never happened. "Get someone to clean this shit up."

"What now?" Pistol Pete asked. He knew that it wouldn't be long until the next wave of Columbian hitmen came through looking for fresh blood.

"I heard of a crazy assassin out in Miami that calls himself, The Black Dragon," Eric said. "I'm going to head out there and see if I can hire him, we'll see how Chico likes it when he sees his loved ones get gunned down."

"Fuck his loved ones!" Jimmy snapped. "We need to hit Chico and let all those Columbian fucks know that we not fucking around."

"If we hit Chico, it'll be an ongoing war between us forever," Eric explained. "But if we take out his loved ones, one by one he'll have no choice but to end this."

"Sounds pretty risky." Pistol Pete said. Killing a cartel leader's family sounded like a death trap.

"You got a better idea?" Eric asked looking around. "I didn't think so," he continued. "I need everyone to lay low for about two weeks get out of town and just stay out of site while this hit man does what he has to do."

"Sorry but I'm not going to be able to take that type of time off," Mike said speaking for the first time. "My boss just told me he's going to need me all week."

"Strap up the best you can and try to keep your head up and your eyes open at all times." Eric warned as he gave Mike a hug.

"What about, Jack?" Jimmy asked. He was still mad that he had let Jack slip through the cracks the last time he had bumped into him.

"Jack is going to have to wait until this, Chico issue is resolved," Eric told him. "Right now I just want you and Murder to get out of town for two weeks and whatever you do stay off the radar. You already know cops will be out looking for us to question us about all the murders at the mansion I already have Mr. Goldberg working on that now. We'll deal with all that when I get back."

# ERIC

# 16

Eric stood in the mirror adjusting his tie. He had moved him and Kelly into one of the rooms at the hotel that he owned and told the manager if anyone came looking for him or asking questions that he hadn't seen or heard from him.

"Are you sure I'm going to be safe here while you're gone?" Kelly asked with a nervous look on her face. The last thing she wanted was for something bad to happen to her husband. Ever since Eric had taken over the family business his heart had turned cold. It was as if he was a totally different person.

"Baby of course you're going to be safe. I'll have four men guarding this door twenty four hours a day until I get back," Eric assured her. "If you need anything, one of my men will be glad to get it for you," Eric paused so he could look Kelly in her eyes. "For no reason what so ever are you to leave this room understand?"

Kelly nodded her head. "Are you sure I'm going to be safe here while you're gone?"

"Yes I shouldn't even be gone for that long."

"When is this going to all be over?" Kelly asked.

"In a few days baby, now I have to go and..."

"I'm talking about for good!" Kelly yelled cutting him off. "I'm sick of this shit! I want my old life back! I want my old husband back!"

"Listen baby," Eric grabbed Kelly's hand. "This is my life now and I need to know that you gon be here with me until the end no matter what."

"I'm leaving you!" Kelly said as tears streamed down her eyes. "I refuse to sit back and watch you get killed... I can't do it I just can't."

"So what, you just gon leave me at a time like this?" Eric asked not believing what he was hearing.

"When you leave all this street shit alone, I'll be right here waiting for you." Kelly said as she stood to her feet and gave Eric a tight hug. "I love you and I always will but I can't sit back and watch you walk straight into the fire, we both know what's on the other end of that door, and it's not pretty."

Eric walked over and grabbed his duffle bag that laid on the floor and sat it on the bed. He pulled out $20,000 and held it out toward Kelly. "Here just know if you take this money there's no coming back between me and you."

Kelly wiped the tears from her eyes and looked down at the money then back up at Eric. "Thank you, but no thank you." She said then exited the hotel room leaving Eric standing there holding a stack of cash in his hand. Eric wanted to stop her but he didn't have no time. Pistol Pete was already outside in the hallway waiting for him, he would just have to deal with this when he got back.

Eric stepped out the room dressed in an all-black Armani suit and a large duffle bag in his hand.

"I just saw, Kelly leave, want me to assign a few men to trail her where ever she goes?" Pistol Pete asked.

Eric waved his hand in a dismissive manner. "Nah I ain't got time for her shit right now. I'll deal with her when I get back." Right now Eric had to be totally focused on the mission at hand not only did he have to worry about the Columbian hit men trying to blow his head off but he also had to worry about the law. Eric and Jimmy's face was all over the news and at the moment, Eric didn't need any setbacks. Him and Pistol Pete hopped in the back of the truck that awaited them curbside.

"I think Miami will be a nice new change of scenery," Pistol Pete said.

"I got some club asshole out in Miami that's been begging me to come out there for months," Eric shook his head. "Wants me to invest in some big night club."

"Don't think that would be a bad investment," Pistol Pete said. "I have about $30,000 I know it's not much but hey it's yours if you need it."

Eric looked over at Pistol Pete and smiled. "If I decide to do this deal, I'll be sure to make you a silent partner."

"My man." Pistol Pete smiled as the two men bumped fist.

# DERRICK

# 17

Derrick stepped foot in the intake area of the jail with a smile on his face. He had just been informed that he made bail. Derrick didn't know what was going on, he was just happy to be being released.

"Get this asshole out of here so all these damn reporters and media can get the fuck out of here!" The sergeant barked with an attitude. He was sick and tired of all the attention that Derrick Mason was bringing to his prison.

Derrick stepped foot out into the hall that led to the exit and was immediately met by his lawyer Mr. Goldberg.

"Hey the judge just set your bail for $400,000 about an hour ago," Mr. Goldberg said. "I put up my own cash to bail you out so be expecting an invoice." As soon Derrick stepped foot outside of the prison he was immediately swarmed by the media. Reporters pushed and shoved to question the infamous Derrick Mason.

"Is it true that there's a hit out on your entire family?" A white female reporter asked shoving a recorder as close to Derrick's mouth as possible.

"Are you afraid for your life?" Another reporter asked.

"Is it right back to business for you Derrick?"

A big security guard pushed his way through the crowd until he reached the Cadillac truck that waited curbside for their arrival. Derrick and Mr. Goldberg quickly slid in the back seat of the truck and it instantly pulled away from the curb in a hurry.

"Now what the hell is going on?" Derrick asked. For the past two weeks, he hadn't been able to get anyone on the phone and it was really starting to piss him off.

"Where do I begin," Mr. Goldberg huffed. "Chico's men found Alvarez's body and put a hit out on the entire family."

"You're joking right?" Derrick said not believing what he had just heard.

"I'm afraid not," Mr. Goldberg said quickly. "A hit squad burned your mansion down to the ground a few days ago. Eric and Jimmy made it out of there alive but over eighty bodies were found; now every cop and agent in the world are looking for them right now."

"Fuck!" Derrick cursed loudly. Just from what Mr. Goldberg just told him he knew that he was fucked. "I don't even have no place to stay."

"Eric owns a hotel. We're headed there now. He's got a suite set up for you I spoke to him an hour ago he told me to tell you that he'll be off the radar for a few days," Mr. Goldberg said. "Everything you need will be at the hotel; money, clothes, security, you name it."

"Aight cool but as soon as you hear word from Eric you tell him I said to call me A.S.A. fucking P," Derrick said as the Cadillac truck pulled up in front of the hotel. Derrick stepped out of the truck and he was immediately met by a member of Eric's security. Derrick was quickly escorted upstairs to his room where the first thing he did was hop in the shower. It had been months since the last time he took a real shower in a real bathroom. Derrick held his head under the faucet and let the water massage his scalp it had been a rough few months but Derrick was built for this business and knew how to survive.

Derrick stepped out the shower, dried off and walked throughout the suite in the nude. On his king sized bed rested a mox-berg pump shot gun along with a dessert eagle he had requested the two weapons from the security that stood outside the door. Derrick was no fool and wasn't big on taking chances. He pulled out his cell phone and called one of his old security friends, a man named Oscar. Oscar used to be one of Derrick's best body guards, but had to quit when a sudden death in the family occurred now with his life in danger. Derrick figured if he was going to have someone watching his back it might as well be Oscar.

"Yo who this!" A deep voice bark into the phone.

"Hey Oscar this Derrick. Can you talk for a second?"

The sound of, Derrick's voice instantly brought a smile to Oscar's face. "Derrick Mason, last I heard they had you under the jail. What did I do to deserve this call?"

"I'm in big trouble Oscar. Some very important people put a hit out me and my family," Derrick told him. "I need a little protection until this thing dies down."

"Man I really wish I could help you but I don't live like that no more," Oscar said in shame. Back in the day, he used to be one of the baddest men on the streets but now he had a wife and a family to think about. "I'm a family man now."

Derrick laughed. "So you finally settled down huh?"

"Had too once my wife got pregnant. She started to put the pressure on me," Oscar joked.

It hurt Derrick to hear that his main man was out of the game, but he respected Oscar's decision. "What type of work are you into now?"

"I'm working security at this club," Oscar said. "But it's funny you called cause I just saw your brother Jack."

Just the mention of Jack's name brought a frown to Derrick's face. "You just saw him right now?"

"Yeah he just walked in the club with two fine ass bitches," Oscar said letting the word "Fine" roll off his tongue. "He looking good too, like he came up on a couple of dollars."

"I'm on way right now whatever you do don't let him leave that club!" Derrick barked into the receiver.

"I got you," Oscar said. "Is something wrong?" He looked down at the phone and saw that Derrick had already hung up.

\*\*\*

Oscar stood close to the VIP section that Jack and his crew occupied. Oscar knew if Derrick told him to keep his eye on Jack it had to be something serious. From first glance, Oscar counted four goons and six women in the VIP section. Back in his day, he would have been able to take on all of them at the same time, but now that he's been out of commission for a while, he wasn't too sure about taking a chance like that. Oscar's phone buzzed notifying him that he just received a text message. He looked down at the screen and read the message from Derrick letting him know that he had just entered the club. Oscar walked over to the bar where he met, Derrick. Behind him stood a heavyset man with dark shades and black leather gloves on his hand. From experience, once Oscar spotted the heavyset man dressed in all black he already knew what time it was. "This gon get messy?"

Derrick nodded his head as he slipped his hands into a pair of black gloves. "Where's the best exit?"

"The side door over behind the stage," Oscar nodded his head over towards the right. "Make it quick and not too messy."

The heavyset man walked over towards the VIP section with his .45 down by his side. He walked up, grabbed the velvet rope that separated the VIP and regular people, and stepped inside the section like it was his VIP section. Immediately a man with a shiny baldhead approached him and placed a strong hand on the big man's chest. "Where the fuck you think you going?"

The heavy set quickly pulled out a gun and shot the baldhead man in the leg.

Blocka!

Immediately partygoers scrambled and stumbled over one another when the sound of the shot echoed over the music. The heavyset man stepped over the bald headed man he aimed his gun at Jack, pulled the trigger, but Jack quickly, and desperately pulled one of the women that sat on his lap in the line of fire forcing her to take the bullet that was meant for him. Jack quickly ran and hopped over the rail, scrambling towards the exit as his crew got involved in the shootout with the heavyset man. Jack ran towards the exit when out of nowhere Derrick tackled him sending the two men tumbling violently down a flight of stairs. Derrick landed on top of Jack and began pistol-whipping him as if he was a stranger instead of his brother. He hit Jack repeatedly until one of Jack's henchmen finally tackled Derrick off of him. The henchman landed two blows to Derrick's face before two shots exploded in his stomach. Derrick tossed the wounded man off of him just as he saw Jack get off the floor and take off in a sprint. Without thinking twice, Derrick opened fire on his brother.

Pow! Pow! Pow!

Jack finally reached the exit when he felt a hot slug tear through the back of his thigh. The pain almost caused him to hit the deck, but he knew if he would have hit the floor, he was as good as dead. Jack willed himself to keep moving he wasn't expecting Jack to run down on him in the club. Jack exited the club, pulled his 9mm from its holster, and ran up to the first car he saw. "Bitch get the fuck out the car!" He yelled as he forcefully snatched a skinny chick out of the driver's seat, roughly tossing her down to the unforgiving concrete. Jack slid down behind the wheel just as Derrick and the heavyset man came spilling out of the club.

Jack gunned the engine as bullet assaulted the car as he pulled recklessly out into the street.

# MIKE

# 18

Mike cruised through the streets in his unmarked police car, silently listening to the consistent tapping of the rain. He had been thinking long and hard, and had finally decided that he no longer wanted to have anything to do with the family business. He was ready for a new chapter in his life. Mike knew that Derrick and Eric wouldn't like his decision, but it was his life and at the moment, he wasn't happy with the way his life was playing out. Mike had thought long and hard about his decision and now it was time to let the rest of the family know. Mike pulled into the parking lot of a small rundown diner at a place that rarely had many customers. He pulled his hood over his head and drew the strings tight before stepping out the car and entering the small diner. Sitting in the back of the diner, Mike spotted Derrick sitting, pretending to be reading a newspaper. Mike sat down across from Derrick and smiled. "Good to see you again old man."

"I'm just glad to be out of jail," Derrick sipped his coffee. "I'm glad you agreed to meet with me. I need you to tell me what the hell is going on."

"They found, Alvarez's body and now there's a hit out on the entire family," Mike said.

"Well I'm back home now so trust and believe I'll get all this shit squared away," Derrick began. "But first I'm going to need you to do a few things for me; first I need to let me know when...."

"I'm out."

"Huh?"

"I said I'm out," Mike repeated. He was tired of living like a criminal it was time for him to move on with his life and start to enjoy all the money he had been risking his life for, for so many years.

"You can't get out at a time like this, the family needs you," Derrick began. "Think about the family."

"Fuck the family!" Mike spat with venom in his tone. "This family has done nothing but stopped my growth as a person."

"Son listen," Derrick said trying to gain back control of the situation. "The family is in a bind right now and we need you more than ever. I know things have been a little rough but think about the family."

"Fuck the family!" Mike growled. "This isn't about family," he said with his face crumbled up. "This is about business and I'm done with both this family and this business!" Mike stood up to leave. Derrick quickly grabbed his arm.

"Son if you walk out that door you're on your own!" Derrick growled standing nose to nose with the man he raised since he was a kid. "You better think hard about what you're about to do!"

Mike flashed a smirk. "It's not personal pop, this is business." He turned and exited the small diner leaving Derrick standing there.

# DERRICK

## 19

Derrick stood in the diner with a sour look on his face as he watched Mike slide into his car and pull out into traffic like a mad man in the pouring rain. A part of him was upset with Mike for abandoning the family at a time like this, but the other part of him understood why. Mike was making the decision he was making. Derrick knew this life could drain a person mentally as well as physically. Derrick went to sit down when he noticed five motorcycles zoom pass in the same direction that Mike had just headed.

"Aw shit!" Derrick cursed as he ran out of the diner into the rain. He quickly hopped behind the wheel and burnt rubber out of his parking spot. Derrick wasn't sure about the five motorcycles at first but when he saw the bikes run a red light, he knew immediately that they were a hit team. He stomped down on the gas blowing through a red light trying to catch up with Mike before it was too late. Derrick beeped the horn like a mad man trying to get Mike's attention as he weaved from lane to lane.

# MIKE

# 20

Mike cruised down the street in complete silence. He felt good about the decision he had just made maybe now he could live a normal life, a life where he didn't have to look over his shoulder every five minutes, a life where maybe he could start a family. As soon as Mike was just starting to feel good about himself his thoughts were interrupted when the sound of a car horn blowing repeatedly grabbed his attention. Mike glanced up at his rear view mirror and spot several motorcycles creeping up on him at a fast speed. Before Mike knew what was going on, his back window shattered forcing him to duck down out of reflexes. Mike quickly stomped down on the brakes causing two of the bikers to crash into his back bumper he then quickly moved his foot from the brake back to the gas pedal. Mike ducked his head down as the sound of rapid gunfire ripped through the air. Mike quickly grabbed his walkie-talkie and called for backup. The heavy rain made it hard for Mike to see clearly. Out of his side mirror, he spotted another motorcycle coming up on his passenger side. Mike quickly cut his wheel to the right forcing the biker to collide straight into a parked car. Just as Mike was starting to feel good about himself, one of the bikers shot out his back tire, which caused the car to swerve out of control. Mike grabbed the wheel with both hands trying to regain control but when he looked up he saw a minivan. "Oh shit!" Mike yelled as his car and the minivan collided like two rams. The air bag exploded violently smacking Mike in the face shattering his nose in the process. Mike lifted his head up in a daze and saw two figures dressed in dark clothes walking towards his car. He could see what was going on, but at the moment, he was too dazed to do something about it. Mike reached down for his gun but froze when he saw Derrick's car run through the two gunmen like bowling pins.

Mike looked over at Derrick and said thank you with his eyes just as Derrick pulled off in a hurry.

# JIMMY

## 21

Jimmy and Cherokee sat camped out in a low-key hotel out in the middle of nowhere in Pennsylvania. It wasn't what Jimmy was used to but it would have to do he was trying to stay off the radar but didn't know how long this would last for. Pennsylvania was cool but Jimmy was used to being around the hustle, ripping, and running. He sat on the couch as he watched Cherokee's head bob slowly up and down on his pole. Cherokee's mouth was wet and loud just as Jimmy liked it. He watched her struggle to try and get the whole thing in her mouth.

Cherokee looked up from in between Jimmy's legs with a seductive look on her face as she let saliva drip sloppily all over his dick. Cherokee worked her hands and mouth a hundred miles an hour until finally Jimmy couldn't take it anymore. He stood up and bent Cherokee over then went up in her forcefully from behind. Cherokee placed her hands on the wall and threw her ass back matching Jimmy's thrust stroke for stroke. Cherokee craned her neck looking back at Jimmy as she bit down on her lip. She enjoyed the site of Jimmy's pole sliding in and out of her.

"This all me?" Jimmy asked as he grabbed a hand full of Cherokee's hair forcing her head to snap back.

"Yes."

"I can't hear you!" Jimmy growled as he slapped Cherokee's ass, making it jiggle.

"Yes."

"I can't hear you!"

"Oh god yes! Yes! Yes!" Cherokee moaned as Jimmy forced her to cum for him yet again. Jimmy grabbed Cherokee's waist firmly and sped up his strokes as he tried to pulverize her insides. "Ugh!" Jimmy groaned as he pulled out and released himself all over Cherokee's huge ass.

"Damn," Jimmy huffed as he headed to the bathroom and cut the shower on. He tried to think about several positive things to take his mind off the fact that he and his girl were hiding in a hotel room out in the middle of nowhere. Jimmy was the hothead in the family and he being stuck up in a room wasn't sitting well with him. He stuck his head under the shower and enjoyed the hot water running down his head and back. Jimmy jumped when he felt a pair of hands rub on his chest from behind.

"It's me baby," Cherokee whispered in Jimmy's ear as she grabbed the soap and began to clean off his penis. "What's on your mind I can tell that something is off."

"I ain't with all this hiding shit," Jimmy said. "I'd rather die like a man instead of hiding like some coward."

"You'll never be a coward baby," Cherokee purred as she washed Jimmy's back. "You just have to be smart and not put yourself in lose-lose situations. Start thinking like a boss."

Jimmy spun around, faced Cherokee, and gripped her ass. "Why you love me so much? I'm no good."

"You may be no good, but you're great for me," Cherokee looked him in the eyes. "When I think of a husband I think of you. You're smart, funny, and you don't take no shit. Did I mention blessed?" She reached down and pulled on his rod. That last statement put a smile on Jimmy's face.

Cherokee stepped out the shower, dried off, and exited the bathroom naked. "Let me take you out tonight."

"Maybe best if we stay inside," Jimmy said drying off the back of his neck with a towel. "What you had in mind?"

"Dinner and a movie," Cherokee stepped into her thong. "It'll be fun."

Jimmy leaned back on the dresser and watched Cherokee wiggle in her jeans. He walked over to the nightstand, grabbed the bottle of liquor, and poured him and Cherokee a shot. Jimmy downed the liquid fire in one quick gulp, and then handed the other shot glass over to Cherokee. She tossed the shot back like a trooper then headed to the bathroom to put on her make up.

Forty-five minutes later, Jimmy and Cherokee stepped into the theater. "Just in time," Cherokee looked up at the screen and saw that the movie was just coming on. Once the couple were seated, Cherokee opened her purse and took out all the snacks that she had snuck in. She didn't care how much money her and Jimmy had, she refused to pay six dollars for some popcorn.

"You mad ratchet," Jimmy joked as he reached for some chips.

Cherokee playfully slapped his hand away. "Nope keep your hands off my ratchet chips."

Jimmy leaned back in his seat and enjoyed the movie. This outing was exactly what he needed. This quality time with Cherokee was refreshing. Jimmy was enjoying the movie until the man sitting behind him kept on talking during the movie. Cherokee could tell that the man talking was bothering Jimmy so she squeezed his hand signaling for him to calm down and relax. Jimmy looked back and saw that it was a man with dreads who had the motor mouth.

"You see," the man with the dreads said, in an outburst. "This the shit I be talking about... watch this white chick fall... what I tell you... they always fall and hurt they leg or some dumb shit."

"Yo can you shut the fuck up!" Jimmy turned around enough was enough he was sick and tired of hearing the man's mouth. "I can't even hear the movie!"

"I paid for my ticket like everyone else!" The man with the dreads shot back. "I can talk if I feel like it... who gon stop me?"

Jimmy's hand moved in a blur as he leaned over and smacked the shit out the man with the dreads then followed with a quick right cross that stunned him. Before Jimmy could hit the man again, he saw Cherokee get two clean punches in on the man with the dreads face. Jimmy sat back for a second and watched Cherokee go to work on the man with dreads. It felt good to know he had a rider on his side. Jimmy stepped in and finished the man off with a belly-to-belly slam from there him and Cherokee stomped the man out until security came and forced them out of the movie theater.

# MIKE

# 22

A week later, Mike stepped out of the car and entered the small diner that he had met Derrick at a few days ago. He didn't want to be there again, but Derrick called him and said it was an emergency, so he decided to see what was up. Sitting in the back of the diner again was none other than Derrick Mason. "What the fuck do you want?"

"Watch your fucking mouth when you talk to me!" Derrick warned with a finger pointed in Mike's face. "Now sit down and listen to what the fuck I have to say!"

Mike reluctantly sat down across from the man that raised him. "You got five minutes." He said with an attitude.

"I saved your life the other day. You owe me," Derrick said with evil smirk on his face.

"As much work as I put in for this family I don't owe you shit!" Mike spat. "All I want is to be free. Why can't you just let me get out and be happy for me?"

"You get out when I say you get out!" Derrick growled. "I raised you since you were a child and this is how you repay me?"

"Why won't you just let me go, huh? Why do you want me to stay in this game until something bad happens to me?"

"Because I need you right now son, that's why," Derrick said. He knew Mike's heart wasn't in the game anymore but he couldn't let something as small as that stop the big picture.

"Fuck you!" Mike said as he stood up and headed for the exit.

"If you don't help me I'll expose you to the media and tell them how big of a part you played in our organization," Derrick threatened with a serious look on his face. "I'll tell them everything," Derrick stood up and walked over, and stood nose to nose with Mike. "You work for me, you always have, and you always will," he smiled. "Nothing personal but business is business."

"What the fuck do you want from me?" Mike growled. He knew that Derrick had him by the nuts not leaving him many options.

"As you know it's been hard for me to move around lately with all the heat on us not to mention these crazy ass Columbians coming out of the wood works," Derrick said. "I have a shipment of guns coming into town in two days it's a big shipment, two cars so I'm going to need someone I can trust to drive one of the cars while I drive the other," Derrick explained. "Don't even worry; the money we make off of these guns will be sure to put a smile on your face."

Mike wanted so badly to break Derrick's face for blackmailing him He couldn't believe that the man he would of given his life for didn't want to see him get out of the game and live a normal life. The more Mike thought about this the more it angered him and made him want to kill Derrick even more. He always knew Derrick had snake ways he just never thought that those ways would have ever been used on him.

"We don't have a problem do we?" Derrick asked with a smirk.

"Nah no problem at all. Can I go now?" Mike asked.

Derrick disrespectfully flicked his wrist in a dismissive manner as he watched Mike exit the diner. He hated to have to play hardball with Mike, but it was crunch time and he didn't really have time to go back and forth with the man he raised from ground up. Right now, Derrick had to figure out how he was going to get his family out of the hole that they were in. All the time he spent in jail was a serious setback but now it was time for him to regain control and get the family back on top.

# JACK

# 23

Jack Mason laid on the couch with his leg propped up. He still couldn't believe that Derrick had shot him in the leg. The last thing Jack wanted was for Derrick to find out it was he behind all of the attacks on the family business. The way Jack had it planned he wanted Derrick and, Jimmy Mason dead. With the muscle out of the way, he figured he'd be able to buy Eric off or either hire him and have him work for him instead. But things didn't go the way he had planned them too. It seemed like every time he had a master plan it would get messed up somehow. Jack knew that with the Columbians hunting the Mason family, it would only be a matter of time before he was the last Mason standing. The ringing of the doorbell snapped Jack back into reality he had totally forgot that he had a meeting with some new up and coming drug dealer named Rico. Jack needed a person on his team that he could depend on to get rid of a large quantity of product and, Rico was perfect. Not only did he have spots that he operated out of all throughout the city he also had a few spots out of town as well.

"Your guests are here," One of Jack's bodyguards announced, leading Rico and another man into the den.

"Gentlemen welcome make yourselves at home," Jack said gesturing for them to sit down with a wave of his hand.

"Nah we'd rather stand," Rico said. He stood in the den dressed in all black, on his feet were a pair of construction timberlands, covering his eyes were a pair of dark shades and a blue Yankee fitted hat sat low on his head almost covering his eyes. "If you don't mind I'd like to get down to business." His partner that stood next to him also wore all black with a serious I don't play no games look on his face.

"I'm willing to give you ten kilos on consignment," Jack began. "You report to me and to me only and every now and then if I need a favor, I'll call you and have your team take care of it for me how does that sound?"

Rico shook his head with a serious look on his face. "I'm not here for consignment. I'll pay for the ten kilos and I'll call you when I'm ready to buy ten more. I don't do favors." He said in a serious tone.

"Listen Rico, I don't think you understand," Jack sat up. "I have a lot of product that I have to get rid of and I heard that you were the man to move this amount of product, you pay for ten kilos, and I'll give you thirty you just pay when you get it. How does that sound? I didn't call you here to nickel and dime."

"Whatever you give me I'll move it," Rico said. At first, he was hesitant to work with Jack. He had heard all the stories about how much of a grease ball he was and planned on staying as far away from him as possible, but with the streets running dry he didn't have too many options on where he could get some work from and at the moment he needed a steady connect.

"That's what I like to hear," Jack smiled. "I'll have one of my workers drop the work off to at a location of your liking."

Rico pulled a pen out of his pocket, scribbled down an address, and handed it to, Jack. "Have it dropped off at that address at 10pm."

Jack nodded. "Will do."

Rico and his sidekick, a man that went by the name; Benny turned and headed for the exit. Once outside, Benny turned and looked at Rico. "I don't trust that motherfucker."

"Me either but it's all good," Rico said in a cool tone. The truth was he never had intention of paying Jack for the extra twenty kilos that he was about to receive. Rico turned and looked at Benny. "Business is business."

# ERIC

# 24

Eric sat on the jet with his eyes closed but he wasn't sleep. No way could he sleep at a time like this. He had no idea what to expect with this meeting between him and The Black Dragon. This guy was supposed to be the best at what he does and if that were true, then this mission would be money well spent. Eric couldn't wait to finally end this silly war and get back to making money because at the end of the day, that's what it was all about. Every time, Eric tried to go to sleep, his mind started thinking about Kelly. He had been trying to call her for the last few hours but every time he called, it went straight to voicemail. Eric knew he was in a dangerous business, a business that on any given day, he could end up with a bullet in the back of his head and it wasn't fair to ask Kelly to fuck up her life just because of him. A part of him understood why she was ignoring his calls. Eric tried to put himself in Kelly's shoes and see where he was coming from.

"You alright over there?" Pistol Pete asked. He could tell that Eric wasn't asleep.

"Yeah, I'm good just got a lot on my mind," Eric admitted. Being the boss was a job that required his immediate attention all the time it was starting to feel like he never had any time for himself anymore or his personal life. If he could go back in time and change things back to the way that they used to be, he would do it in a flash.

"Once we holla at, The Black Dragon and get Chico off our backs things will go back to normal," Pistol Pete told him. He had no idea how things were going to play out. All Pistol Pete could do was keep his fingers crossed.

Eric and Pistol Pete stepped off the jet and into the tinted out truck that awaited them. "When we get there make sure you watch my back this guy is supposed to be the real deal." Eric had been responding back and forth with the assassin over email but for some reason, The Black Dragon refused to use a phone so it was kind of as if they were going into the situation blindly.

Pete nodded his head. "I got you."

Twenty minutes later the truck pulled up in front of a nice looking building. Eric read the numbers on the front of the building and looked at Pistol Pete. "Yeah this the right building." The two men entered the building and pushed the call button for the elevator. When the elevator arrived, both men stepped on with nervous looks on their faces not because they were scared but because they didn't know what to expect. Eric stepped off the elevator and walked down the hall until they reached the apartment they were looking for. Eric took a deep breath, raised his fist, and knocked on the door. He waited a few seconds before he knocked again. Eric went to knock on the door again, when the apartment behind him door swung open. Eric and Pistol Pete spun around to find themselves looking down the barrel of two silenced guns.

A dark skin fit man dressed in a snug fitting black uniform stood with a silenced gun in each hand. "Who the fuck are ya'll?"

# DERRICK

## 25

Derrick Mason sat in the passenger seat of the Benz and stared out the window with a grin on his face. He was happy to be a free man again, and with Eric taking care of the Chico situation, he knew it wouldn't be long until he was on top again. Today Derrick was meeting his gun supplier out in the middle of nowhere he needed a lot of guns especially if he was going to war. As the Benz slowed to a stop, Derrick saw his gun connect standing, leaning up against the hood of his van. Derrick stepped out of the Benz with a smile on his face dressed in an expensive suit. "Hey Henry, it's good to see you again," he said as the two men shook hands.

"You're twenty minutes late. I was just about to leave," Henry said with an attitude. He was anxious to unload all of the guns he had in the back of his van. Henry liked doing business with Derrick he just wished that he'd show up on time, but the money he made, made it all worth it.

"Got caught in traffic," Derrick lied. "For as much money as I pay you, you sure do a lot of complaining."

Henry walked around to the other side of the van and slid the side door open. "Here are your guns, let me get my money so I can be going." He liked Derrick but he didn't like being a sitting duck especially when he was riding dirty.

"Why you in such a rush?" Derrick asked looking Henry up and down.

"Not trying to be sitting around here with a vehicle full of guns out in the open," Henry spat.

Derrick's driver walked back to the Benz then returned carrying a briefcase. "Here's your money," Derrick handed the briefcase over to Henry. "Now help my driver load these guns into my trunk."

"All these guns not going to fit in that trunk," Henry said.

"Hush, my son is coming with a second car. He should be here any minute," Derrick said as he slid a cigar in between his lips and lit it up. He blew out a ring of smoke when he looked up and saw two cars headed in his direction from a distance.

The two cars pulled up side by side and just stood there for a while. Seconds later, Mike hopped out with his gun drawn. "Freeze!" He yelled. "You're under arrest!" All four doors on the second car swung open and four detective's hopped out with their weapons drawn. Seconds later, a helicopter hovered over the vehicles.

"On the ground now!" Mike yelled. Out the corner of his eye, he saw Derrick's driver reaching inside his suit jacket without thinking twice, Mike quickly put him down with three shots to the chest. "Get on the ground now or else you're next!" Mike warned with his gun trained on Derrick. He hoped and prayed that Derrick made a wrong move so he could have a reason to put a bullet in Derrick's ass.

Derrick slowly dropped down to his knees and placed his hands on his head. "You making a big mistake," Derrick growled. "I think you may want to rethink this," he could tell that Mike was moving off of emotion and really didn't think this out.

"You mad?" Mike whispered in Derrick's ear as he slipped the cuffs on his wrist. He growled as he roughly pulled Derrick up to his feet and slammed him against the car. Mike smiled as he gave Derrick a hard gut punch that forced him to double over in pain then forced Derrick to look him in the eyes. "I told you I wanted out but you wouldn't listen!"

Derrick looked, Mike in the eyes. "You just killed yourself you idiot. You're forgetting that I know all your secrets,"

Mike roughly shoved, Derrick in the back of the unmarked car. "This ain't business this is personal motherfucker!" Mike growled then slammed the door shut.

# ERIC

# 26

"I'm Eric and this here is my partner Pistol Pete," Eric said with his hands raised. "I'm looking for The Black Dragon."

The man dressed in all black kept both of his guns trained on the two men that stood before him. "Remove your weapons slowly and place them on the floor." He watched as Eric and Pistol Pete did as they were told.

"Now kick them over to me," the man dressed in all black ordered. Eric slowly kicked both of the guns over towards the man.

The man placed one of his silenced gun in its holster, then bent down and picked the two guns up from off the floor. He tossed the guns behind him inside the apartment and holstered his other gun. "Nice to meet you gentlemen," he extended his hand. "I'm The Black Dragon."

The men shook hands, and then The Black Dragon invited them inside of the apartment. "Sorry about that, but you can never be too careful. Now how can I help you two gentlemen?"

"I would like to hire you to take out the family of a very powerful man," Eric began. "I'm in the middle of a war right now and the only way to stop it is let the other side know that the war isn't one sided. Each day this war goes on the more money and bodies I lose," Eric explained.

"How many bodies are you asking for?" The Black Dragon asked. He needed a head count so he could know how much to charge. "And who is the target?"

"The target is a man that goes by the name Chico, and he's a cartel leader out in Columbia," Eric informed. He knew a job like this would be pricey, and not to mention difficult with the amount of security that more than likely guarded Chico's estate.

"I need a head count." The Black Dragon said in a smooth tone.

"Two-to-five bodies should be good," Eric said. "I want the people that's the most close to him taken out."

"But not Chico?"

"No not Chico, just the people closest to him," Eric said. He knew that by hitting Chico's loved ones it would definitely let Chico know that he wasn't fucking around and meant business besides. Chico was the only one that could call the war off if Chico was killed then the war would more than likely continue on forever.

"My price is three million," The Black Dragon said without blinking an eye. He knew that in order to kill two-to-five of Chico's closest family members that he would more than likely have to kill over thirty-to-forty guards first just in order to get them.

Eric's face crumbled up. "Don't you think that price is a little steep?"

"My price is my price," The Black Dragon said with a straight face. "Depends on how bad you want this job done. It's up to you either you take it or leave it."

"Can I have a second to talk it over with my partner?" Eric stood to his feet.

The Black Dragon nodded as he watched Eric and Pistol Pete step off to the side and talk in hushed tones.

"His prices are way higher than I expected," Eric admitted. "Plus what happens if he can't get the job done?"

"You gotta pay to play," Pistol Pete countered. "Even if he can't get the job done at least Chico will still get the message that we not just sitting back waiting for him to kill us."

"Good point," Eric said. He knew without risk there would be no reward and at the moment, he didn't really have too many options to choose from. Eric walked back over to The Black Dragon and looked him in the eyes. "Are you sure you can get the job done?"

The Black Dragon kept a straight face and replied. "I'm positive I can get the job done. This is what I do."

"You're hired," Eric said as the two men shook hands and closed the agreement.

# JIMMY

# 27

**"**Oh yes, right there baby!" Cherokee purred as she grabbed a fistful of the sheets on the bed. In between her thick thighs was Jimmy's head and he was using his tongue as a deadly weapon. Jimmy slurped, licked, and kissed all over Cherokee's love box. While eating Cherokee like a mad man, Jimmy slipped two fingers inside of her in an attempt to make her orgasm even more explosive. Seconds later, Cherokee's body began to tremble as her legs locked firmly around Jimmy's head and ears. She tried to escape from Jimmy, but he held on tight and he continue to suck on her clit as if he needed it to live. Cherokee gasped for air as she finally disconnected Jimmy's face from in between her thighs. "You are a fucking animal!"

Jimmy wiped his mouth with a smile on his face as he grabbed the bottle of Grey Goose that rested on the nightstand and turned it up to his lips. Jimmy was getting ready to go in for round two when he heard his phone vibrating on the nightstand. Normally, Jimmy would have ignored his phone but since he knew that the family was in a tight situation, he decided to answer it. "Yo," he answered.

"Jimmy it's me."

"Pop?" Jimmy asked. He could barely hear due to all the noise in the background.

"Yeah it's me!" Derrick's voice barked through the line. "I'm in jail!"

"What?" Jimmy asked with a confused look on his face. "What happened?"

"Mike has turned on the family," Derrick said in a serious tone. "I need you son."

"Say no more I'll take care of it," Jimmy said as he hung up the phone. Jimmy knew exactly what Derrick was asking him to do the only problem was he still had a lot of love for Mike. The two men grew up in the same house and were brothers for as long as he could remember.

"You alright baby?" Cherokee asked. "Looks like you just saw a ghost.

"Pack your things baby we going back to New York tonight."

# MILLIE

# 28

Millie sat in her cell with a sad look on her face. After the brawl with Ebony in the shower room a C.O. That was on Millie's payroll made it look like Millie's best friend Pam was in the brawl and not Millie. Pam decided to take one for the team so Millie wouldn't lose her release date. Sitting on Millie's lap was a letter from Mike, but of course he didn't mail the letter off in his own name. Inside the letter, he had broken down everything to Millie from how he had asked Derrick several times to let him go on and live a normal life. Ever since Mike was a child he had always loved and respected Millie she was the reason why he had joined the police academy in the first place she was also the reason he had joined the family business. It was Millie who saw something special in him from day one. It saddened her to know that no matter how much she loved Mike that he had to go. Snitching was something that she didn't tolerate nor condone, and if Millie were on the streets, she would have taken his life herself. She shook her head with a disgusted look on her face; ever since Millie had been incarcerated, she noticed that her entire family had been falling apart. "I gotta hurry up and get out of here and get things back in order," she said to herself as she stepped out of her cell and headed down to the TV room so she could stretch her legs. Millie made it downstairs when two correction officers stopped her and threw her against the wall and began to frisk her. "Fuck is this all about?"

The two correction officers didn't answer Millie, they just handcuffed her and made her sit Indian-style on the floor. Millie sat on the floor as she watched several correction officers storm in her cell. She could hear them tearing her cell apart looking for some form of contraband. After a forty-minute search, the C.O.'s were upset that they didn't find anything. Millie made sure she had her cell cleaned out after the big fight with Ebony. She had a feeling that the officers would be coming for her. A heavyset C.O. roughly pulled Millie up to her feet by her arm and forced her down the hall. "Where ya'll taking me?" Millie asked but got no answer. After a brief walk, the C.O. led Millie into the warden's office.

"Have a seat," The Warden said nodding towards the chair that sat directly in front from her desk. "So from what I hear you haven't learned nothing from being inside my prison," the warden said with a mean look on her face. "You've been running drugs in my prison all this time right under my nose."

"Huh?" Millie said with her face crumbled up faking ignorance. From what the warden was, saying, it only meant one thing; that someone had been talking.

"Don't play stupid with me!" the warden yelled with a finger pointed at Millie. "How were you getting your drugs in here?"

"What drugs?"

"I swear to god if you don't tell me something I'll make your last few months in here a living hell!" the warden threatened.

"I really wish I could help you warden but I have no idea or knowledge of what you're talking about," Millie said with a straight face. She knew that the warden was just fishing for information and didn't have any concrete evidence to hold her on. "May I go back to my cell now?"

"Take this bitch to the box," The Warden ordered. "And make sure she stays there until it's time for her to be released."

# JIMMY

## 29

Jimmy sat in the passenger seat of the Benz bobbing his head slowly to the music that pumped through the speakers as the rain tapped loudly against the windshield. Tonight, he wasn't dressed in one of his expensive suits instead he rocked a pair of black jeans, black steel toe boots, and a black thermal shirt, on his head was a black skully and on his lap rested a P90. Jimmy slipped his hands inside a pair of latex gloves and began to screw the silencer on the barrel of the handgun.

"That's fucked up that Mike went out like that," Murder said, keeping his eyes focused on the road. "I still can't believe that shit."

"It is what it is," Jimmy said with a serious look on his face. He needed to be focused for this job; he and Mike were brothers and had been close for over twenty years. Now the same man that he once used to play in the sandbox with was the same man that he was about to murder.

Murder pulled up across the street from Mike's apartment and killed the lights. "You sure you don't want me to handle this one?" He asked since he knew how close Jimmy and Mike were. Murder knew something like this had to be hard for Jimmy.

"Nah I have to do this myself," Jimmy said as he stepped out the car and jogged across the street and entered Mike's building. Jimmy entered the building and trotted up to the third floor. He stepped out into the hallway with a two-handed grip on his gun as he eased down the hall. When Jimmy reached the front door, he shot the locks off and let himself in. Inside the apartment was dark but the light from the TV could be seen shining from the backroom. Jimmy slowly eased his way towards the back room. The closer he got to the backroom the louder the TV could be heard. Jimmy reached the backroom and slowly stepped inside with the business end of his gun leading the way. Jimmy looked around the room and at first glance, it appeared to be empty. But just as he was about to check the closet he felt the cold steel of a gun barrel being pressed into the back of his head.

"Drop the gun now!" Mike growled in Jimmy's ear. Jimmy slowly dropped the gun down to the floor. "Kick it across the room."

Jimmy slowly raised his hands and kicked the gun out of arms reach.

"So the old man sent you huh?" Mike said, as he patted Jimmy down and removed his back up weapon. "Sit down on the bed!" Mike ordered.

"So why'd you do it?" Jimmy asked. "Why'd you rat out pops?"

"I told that cocksucker I wanted out and he threatened to blackmail me," Mike shrugged. "But I'd rather sit in a cell for the rest of my life before I live on my knees. So Derrick can tell the media whatever he wants. I could care less; I'm at peace with myself."

"Listen it's not too late to make things right," Jimmy said thinking of a way to kill Mike without using a weapon. "Let me help you."

Mike looked at Jimmy and smiled. "I've known you all my life. I know when you're full of shit," he said as he pulled out his phone and called in for back up. "Just keep cool and in five minutes this will be all over."

"You putting me in jail isn't going to stop anything," Jimmy said in a calm tone. "You're still a dead man and you know it."

Mike looked at Jimmy and gave him a sad look. "Don't you realize we're all dead, there are no winners in this game this game ain't nothing but a trap. I can't believe I was dumb enough to stay involved this long I should of been got out!"

"Ain't no getting out Mike, you know the rules," Jimmy looked him dead in the eyes. "Now put that gun down while you still have a chance to fix this."

\*\*\*

Downstairs Murder sat behind the wheel, texting some new girl he'd just met, when he spotted a police car pull up in front of Mike's building. "Shit!" He cursed as he grabbed his 9mm from off his lap and stepped out the Benz out into the rain. Murder crept up on the two officers from behind and put a bullet in the back of both of their heads, killing them on the spot. Murder then quickly jogged back over to the Benz. "Come Jimmy hurry up," he whispered to himself as he looked for any sign of any more cops.

\*\*\*

"What the fuck?" Mike said out loud when he heard the two thunderous gunshots ring out coming from downstairs.

Once Jimmy heard the gunshots, he quickly made his move. Without warning, Jimmy rushed Mike and tackled him down to the floor. As the two bothers wrestled and fought over the gun, it discharged several times by mistake putting huge holes in the wall. Jimmy landed two vicious blows to Mike's chin forcing him to drop the gun. Jimmy quickly rolled off of Mike, scooped his gun up from off the floor, and came up firing.

Pst! Pst! Pst! Pst!

Mike swiftly rolled to his feet and took off around the corner just as four bullets decorated the wall just above his head.

Jimmy placed his back up against the wall with a two-handed grip on his silenced weapon. He sprung from behind the wall only to see the front door left wide open. Jimmy ran out into the hallway and stopped short when he looked down and saw a trail of blood dots on the floor. He followed the trail over towards the staircase before he could grab the door handle, the door flung open. Jimmy halfway squeezed down on the trigger but stopped when he saw Murder step out into the hallway. "Did you see him?"

"Nah he must of ran upstairs cause he ain't pass me," Murder said breathing heavily.

"Come on let's go catch this mother fucker. He's been hit," Jimmy said with excitement nodding down towards the blood trail.

"We gon have to do that another day. I got two dead cops downstairs and more on the way," Murder said quickly.

"Fuck!" Jimmy cursed as him and Murder abandoned the mission and ran down the stairs skipping two and three steps at a time. They spilled out the building like mad men and quickly hopped in the Benz and peeled off.

# DERRICK

# 30

Derrick laid on his cot staring up at the ceiling with an aggravated look on his face. He was still upset and couldn't believe that Mike, the same man he had raised since he was a child, had put him in jail. It didn't feel right when Derrick put the hit out on him, but Mike had left him no choice. The situation still didn't seem real; it needed a little more time to settle in. The more Derrick stared up at the ceiling, the angrier he became. Prison was starting to feel more like home then a place where, he tried his hardest to stay out of. At a time like this, it seemed as if anything that could go wrong did go wrong and if it weren't for bad luck, he wouldn't have no luck at all. Since his arrest, Derrick refused to eat the nasty prison food; at the moment food was the last thing on his mind right now his main focus was on finding a way to get back on the streets as soon as possible. Derrick replayed Mike arresting him over and over in his head and wished he had been more prepared. If Derrick were thinking straight, Mike would have never been able to get the drop on him the way he did. Now his only options were to either, spill the beans and tell the world about Mike's involvement in the family business, or kill him. After giving the decision a lot of thought, Derrick decided it would be best to have Mike murdered, rather than go out like a chump and snitch on him. Derrick would be allowed to use the phone in a few hours and he couldn't wait to call Jimmy and find out if he had taken care of business. Derrick's thoughts were interrupted when he heard his cell door crack open. He immediately shot to his feet expecting the worst. Derrick didn't become an O.G. by being stupid he didn't know what to expect but he was prepared for whatever. Just as Derrick was about to go peek his head out of his cell and see what was going on, a Columbian man with a long ponytail ran up in Derrick's cell screaming with a shank in his hand. The Columbian man swung the shank with bad intentions and sliced Derrick across his chest. The Columbian went to land another knife strike when Derrick caught him with a quick left hook that snapped The Columbian man's head to the left. Derrick quickly grabbed The Columbian man's knife hand as the two fought and struggled for possession of the knife as they tore the small cell up in the process. They both tossed each other against the wall back and forth before Derrick kneed The Columbian man in the groin as the two men went spilling out of the cell on to the tier. The Columbian man landed a vicious head butt that instantly drew blood from Derrick's nose. Derrick went to grab his nose and, the Columbian didn't waste any time jamming the knife into Derrick's shoulder all the way to the handle.

"Arghhh!" Derrick screamed in pain as he felt the sharp blade pierce through his flesh. The Columbian tried to take advantage of the situation and land a powerful right hook, but Derrick ducked the punch just in time and used the Columbian's momentum to toss him over the banister and off the top tier. Several other inmates cooed with a loud, "ooooooooooh!" When they saw The Columbian man's body smack violently onto the floor.

"Shit!" Derrick growled as he snatched the knife out of his shoulder and tossed it on the floor. Before Derrick could do anything else, he was roughly tackled down to the floor by several big correction officers. One officer placed his knee on the back of Derrick's neck while his partners handcuffed him and dragged him away yelling and screaming.

# MIKE

# 31

Mike laid in the hospital bed with a stressed out look on his face. At the foot of his bed sitting in a foldout chair was another detective questioning him. The detective was asking the same questions over and over again but in different ways and it was really beginning to piss Mike off.

"Listen man. I told you over and over again that Jimmy Mason broke into my house and tried to kill me. I fought him off and barely escaped with my life."

"Any reason why Jimmy Mason would want you killed?" The detective asked with a raised brow. "I mean if he went through all the trouble to break into your home and try to kill you it has to be for a reason."

"Well I wish I could have stayed and asked him but I was too busy trying to dodge bullets," Mike said sarcastically. He was tired of being interrogated and was ready to be released from the hospital."

"Thank you for your cooperation detective Brown," the detective said as he finally stood up and exited the room leaving Mike all alone with just him and his thoughts.

Mike winced in pain as he sat up and looked down at his watch. Every cop in world was already looking for Jimmy, so he knew it would only be a matter of time before he was caught. Now it was time to focus on getting rid of Eric. Mike felt bad about putting the entire family in jail, but he had no choice as long the Mason family was free and alive they wouldn't stop coming for him until he was no longer breathing that's why he had to strategically take out each member of the family one by one. The good thing about the situation was that Mike knew all of the family's secrets and was willing to use that to his advantage. Derrick was already in jail, Jimmy was on his way to jail, and now all that was left was Eric.

# ERIC

# 32

Eric stepped foot into the empty nightclub with Pistol Pete right behind him. It was three o'clock in the afternoon and the club wasn't scheduled to open for hours. Eric and Pistol Pete weren't there to party; instead, they were there because the owner invited them to the club so they could talk business. Eric approached the bar and spotted a beautiful Latin woman cleaning a few glasses; her long wavy hair was pinned up in a sloppy bun. "Excuse me; I'm looking for Winston, would you happen to know where I can find him."

"Sure," The Latin woman said with a bright smile on her face. "Give me one second and I'll go get him for you."

"Thank you," Eric said as he watched the woman's ass switch all the way upstairs. "Damn, Miami might not be that bad after all."

Two minutes later Winston walked down stairs dressed in a gray suit, the top four buttons on his dress shirt were left unbuttoned, showing off two thin gold chains that hugged his neck. "Gentlemen it's nice to meet you," Winston said with a smile as he extended his hand.

"Pleasures all mines," Eric gave Winston's hand a firm grip.

"If you gentlemen don't mind, would you follow me to my office?" Winston led Eric and Pistol Pete upstairs to his office and poured three strong drinks. "Okay so I'm not going to waste you guys time. I'm going to get straight to it," he handed both men their drinks. "I want you to invest in my club," Winston said looking at Eric. "I want you to be a silent partner this will be a great investment for you because you'll see an instant return on your investment."

"Well if business is doing so well then what do you need me for?" Eric raised his glass up to his lips and took a sip.

"Well it's like this. I want to buy a few supermarkets, but I don't have the cash handy," Winston explained. "So the money you invest will make us 50/50 partners and I'll use that capital to get my supermarkets. Sounds like a win-win to me, not to mention, I'm sure I'll be able to learn so much working beside a business mastermind like yourself." Winston knew all about the Mason family. He had done his research and became very fond of Eric Mason and his business endeavors. By doing research, Winston realized that it was Eric Mason's businesses that really put the Mason family on top. With all of Eric's businesses, the Mason family was able to clean boatloads of drug money and Winston wanted a person like that on his team.

"I don't know too much about Miami so I'll have to think about it," Eric sipped his drink. "I'm sure you've heard about my family's reputation."

"Why yes of course I have," Winston answered quickly.

"Good because the first sign of any shady business from you and I'll have your brains blow out and mailed to your family," Eric said looking Winston straight in the eyes. "I'll be in touch," he said as him and Pistol Pete stood then headed for the exit. Once outside the club, Pistol Pete spoke freely. "What you think? Does it sound like a good deal?"

"Not for me," Eric paused. "But it sounds like a good deal for you."

"Yeah right, I wish I had that type of cash laying around," Pistol Pete chuckled feeling a little embarrassed that his money wasn't as long as it should have been.

"I don't want nothing to do with that club," Eric said in a serious tone. "But what I am going to do is put up the money for you." He looked at Pistol Pete and flashed a smile. "Congratulations, you are about to be a club owner."

"Nah I can't take that much money from you," Pistol Pete waved him off. His pride wouldn't allow him to take Eric's money Pistol Pete was from the old school.

"This is nonnegotiable," Eric said quickly. "It's free money all you have to do is let Winston do all the work while you collect free money maybe go check on the club twice a year just so your face can be seen here and there and you'll be good."

"Thank you so much Eric, I really appreciate all this, and I promise I'll work this debt off cause as you know, I won't be able to sleep until I pay you back every penny." Pistol Pete said.

"I'll have Mr. Goldberg fly out here in a few days and get all the paper work squared away," Eric winked. "You are now officially a business man, congratulations."

# THE BLACK DRAGON

# 33

The tall, muscular Colombian guard walked back and forth with his A.K. resting on his shoulder. A cigarette hung loosely from his lips as he scanned the area. He loved his job especially since he knew there wouldn't be anyone crazy enough to ever try and attack Chico at his mansion, so in his eyes, this was free money. The guard leaned up against the iron gate, removed a flask from his pocket, and enjoy himself a sip of vodka. He went to take another pull from his cigarette when a gloved hand roughly covered his mouth as a sharp icepick was forced repeatedly down into his neck, spilling blood everywhere. The Black Dragon quickly dragged the guard's body over into the bushes where he was sure that no one would find it at this time of night. The Black Dragon quickly glanced over both shoulder before hopping the iron gate. He landed on his feet, removed his silenced 9mm from its holster, and inched his way towards the front of the mansion. The Black Dragon made his way towards the front door when out of nowhere, the front door opened, and two guards stepped out. The Black Dragon quickly put the two guards down with headshots. Before he had a chance to move their bodies, another guard came around the corner followed by a canine dog.

"Hey!" The guard yelled before a bullet hit him right between the eyes. When the canine spotted the guard drop to the ground, he quickly took off in the direction of the assassin with his sharp teeth showing. Without hesitation, the Black Dragon raised his silenced weapon and blew half of the dogs face off.

Pst!

The Black Dragon slammed a fresh clip in the base of his gun and then entered the mansion. He stepped foot inside and quickly hid behind a statue as three guards came running towards the front door. The Black Dragon patiently waited for the trio to run past him before he sprung from behind the statue and put all three gunmen down with headshots. He moved throughout the mansion with the stealth of a cat burglar. The Black Dragon crept up on another guard from behind, grabbed him, and slit his throat from ear to ear before the guard's body hit the floor. The Black Dragon felt a fist smash into the back of his head from behind. The blow staggered him but didn't drop him. The Black Dragon spun and saw the guard raising his A.K. He quickly took off in a sprint as the guard squeezed down on the trigger and swayed his arms back and forth. The Black Dragon ran as fast as he could and dived out into the hallway just as bullets decorated the wall right where his head used to be. The guard kept his finger down on the trigger as he followed the Black Dragon out into the hallway, when the guard stepped out into the hall the assassin was nowhere to be found.

"Shit!" The guard mumbled under his breath as he slowly inched his way down the hall, he heard a noise behind him, and then suddenly his feet were swept out from under him. The guard's head bounced violently off the hardwood floor. Just as the Black Dragon readied to put a bullet in the guard's head, he felt a strong pair of arms grab him from behind in a bear hug. He quickly pushed himself backwards and rammed the guard's back into the wall. From there, the Black Dragon delivered an elbow to the guard's rib, and then hip tossed him down to the hardwood floor. Before he could finish the guard off the other guard peeled himself up off the floor and charged the assassin. The guard hit the Black Dragon hard and lifted him off his feet as the two men went crashing through the door of one of the guest rooms. The Black Dragon made it to his feet and delivered a lightning-fast eight-punch combination that left the guard's face a bloody mess. He then finished him off with a crushing openhanded blow to the nose. Before the guard's body even hit the floor, the other guard entered the room swinging with bad intentions. The Black Dragon easily weaved five punches back to back, and then landed two punches of his own. From the way that the guard took the punches, the Black Dragon could tell that the man standing before him couldn't take his power. The Black Dragon landed a jab that violently snapped the guard's head back he went to finish the guard off with a roundhouse kick to the face, but the guard caught his leg along with the rest of his body in midair and forcefully slammed him down to the floor. The guard climbed on top of the assassin and started raining blows down on his face. "Yeah motherfucker! What's up now?" He growled as he unloaded on the assassin.

The Black Dragon took the first two punches well, but on the third punch, he caught the guard's arm and slipped it into an armbar. He applied pressure on the guard's arm until he heard it snap.

Crunch!

"Urrrgh!" The guard howled in pain as he felt the assassin slip behind him and put him a chokehold. The Black Dragon violent snapped the guard's neck, and then tossed the man's body to the floor as if it was trash. He pulled his back up gun from his leg holster and continued on throughout the mansion.

\*\*\*

Chico and his daughter's mother laid in the bed watching a new web series called, *The Hand I Was Dealt*. He had been hearing about the series, but this was his first time actually getting around to watching it and he had to admit that it was very good from the first episode. The web series was interrupted when a loud series of gunshots ripped through the air.

Chico quickly jumped out of bed and grabbed the dessert eagle that rested under his pillow. The first thing that came to his mind was to protect his daughter who was asleep in her room down the hall. Chico snatched his bedroom door open and froze when he saw a gunman holding a gun to his eight-year-old daughter's head.

"Whoa!" Chico said raising his hands in surrender. "Listen man I don't know who you are but if you want money I have plenty of it. It's yours just let the girl go."

"I was sent by Eric Mason. He asked me to deliver a message," The Black Dragon said as he pressed the barrel of his gun even further into the back of the little girl's skull. "Drop your weapon."

Chico quickly laid his gun down on the floor. "Whatever you want just don't hurt my daughter," he pleaded.

"Eric Mason asked that you call the hit off or else everyday one of your love one's will die!" The

Black Dragon said. "If you do not agree with these terms trust and believe you will be seeing me again."

"I'll do whatever you want just please don't hurt my daughter," Chico begged.

"Call the hit off...now!"

Chico slowly grabbed his cell phone and made a call. "Yeah it's me leave the Mason family alone. The hit is off!" He yelled into his cell phone. "Call it off!"

"You sure boss because we have eyes on Eric Mason right now and he's only with one other guy. I can take him out right now if you want?" The caller on the other end said.

"I said the hit is off, do you hear me? It's off bring all the troops back home!" Chico yelled then ended the call.

The Black Dragon looked Chico in the eyes and pulled the trigger as Chico's daughter's lifeless body crumbled down to the floor.

Boc!

"Noooo!" Chico yelled.

The Black Dragon then lowered his gun and shot Chico in the leg. He then turned his gun on Chico's girlfriend and put a bullet right in the middle of her forehead. "Leave the Mason family alone because trust and believe me, you don't ever want to see my face again!" The Black Dragon growled before he disappeared out of the bedroom leaving Chico laid on the floor with a bullet in his leg and a lot to think about.

# JIMMY

# 34

Jimmy Mason laid on the bed in his hotel room staring up at the ceiling. Every cop in the world was looking for him, not to mention he still feared for his life. Yeah Eric had called him and told him that the bounty on the Mason family's head had been removed, but Jimmy didn't trust Chico or the rest of those Colombian assholes.

The bathroom door opened and Cherokee stepped out dressed in a nice form fitting, tight black dress. She sat on the bed next to Jimmy and rubbed his back. "Don't worry about nothing baby. Everything is going to be okay." She said. "The lawyer said that you'll only be in there for 72 hours, max."

"Yeah I know but that Columbian fuck, Chico has hitters everywhere, especially on the inside," Jimmy said. He had heard about how one of those Columbian hitmen had tried to take out Derrick while he was on the inside and knew there were plenty of more Columbian hitmen on lock down likely waiting for him to show up.

"You're going to be fine and I'll be right here on the outside waiting for you when you get out," Cherokee leaned forward and kissed him on the lips. Jimmy sat up when he heard a knock at the door. He quickly grabbed his .45 from off the nightstand and made his way over to the door. Jimmy peeked through the peephole, then opened the door and stepped to the side. Mr. Goldberg stepped inside the room with a pleasant look on his face. "How you feeling today Jimmy?"

"Like shit!" Jimmy capped back. Today he was turning himself in to the police, something he vowed that he would never do.

"All that the cops have is speculation," Mr. Goldberg began. "And even if what Mike is saying is true, they would have to prove that."

"You sure I'll be getting right back out?" Jimmy asked with a nervous look on his face. Jail was the last place that anyone wanted to be especially by choice.

"Positive," Mr. Goldberg said with a smirk on his face. "You are innocent until proven guilty, besides all they really want to do is question you about all those bodies they found left behind at the Mason family's mansion. You'll more than likely be out by tonight. I just said 72 hours as worst case scenario."

"Come on, let's go and get this over with," Jimmy huffed.

# JACK MASON

# 35

Jack Mason sat in his powder-blue Benz with the top down; talking to some white girl with long blonde hair and breasts that she paid for, which were the size of baby watermelons. He had been enjoying his life and enjoying his wealth even more. Jack let his hand slip down to the white girl's ass as he kicked his best super fly game he could think of. "So how about you go out with me for dinner to tonight?"

"I don't know," the white girl said.

"You don't know?" Jack echoed with his face crumbled up. "You've tried the rest now it's time for you to try the best," he spoke in a fast pitch pimp like tone his hand was now creeping inside the back of the white girl's shorts. Jack was about to say something else, but he paused when he spotted a diesel guy making his way in his direction. Jack squinted his eyes to get a better look and the closer the man got the more familiar he looked. Jack reached under the seat and gripped the handle of the 9mm that rested under the driver's seat.

"Yo Jack, what up? I thought that was you!" The diesel man said with excitement. "It's me Kaine, we did time together over in C-block."

"Oh Kaine, what up? I thought you looked mad familiar," Jack said he knew he had knew the man from somewhere he just couldn't put it together. Jack released the handle of the 9mm and gave Kaine dap. "When you get out?"

"I been out for a minute now, but what's good with you? I see you shinning. I been hearing some good things about you fam," Kaine smiled he then turned his attention on the snow bunny with the big titties that stood by the car. "This you right here?"

"Something like that," Jack said with a smile. "But check it, let me get your math so I can hit you up cause I don't want to be rude," he nodded towards the white girl.

"Definitely," Kaine reached down into his waistband, pulled out a big ass gun, and aimed it in Jack's face. "Nigga you know what the fuck this is!" He yelled as he turned and backslapped the white girl down to the floor. "This a nice ass ride, let me get that!"

Jack thought about reaching for his gun that rested under the seat but he knew Kaine from doing time with him and knew that if he made any sudden movement that Kaine would leave his brains in the passenger seat of his new Benz. "You got it big man."

"I know I got it motherfucker!" Kaine barked as he roughly grabbed Jack by the back of his neck and snatched him out the car. "I never liked ya bitch ass!" He looked down at the Rolex that was on Jack's wrist. "That's a nice watch; I always wanted one of those."

Jack sucked his teeth, removed the watch, and handed it to Kaine. "Listen, I'm a very powerful man now. If you just leave now I'll forget that this ever happened."

Kaine looked at Jack as if he was insane. "What?" With the quickness of a snake, he smacked Jack across the face with his gun.

Whack!

"That's a nice suit you got on too," Kaine smiled. "Take that shit off!"

Jack held his bloody eye as he slowly took off his suit. He had never been this embarrassed in his entire life.

"Oh word, those Polo boxers?" Kaine said with a smirk. "I need those too fam."

"Come on man, you already got all my shit. Can I at least keep my draws?" Jack pleaded with begging eyes.

"What the fuck I just say?" Kaine barked as he backslapped Jack across the face with the gun then roughly ripped Jack's draws off. Kaine didn't want Jack's clothes or his draws he just wanted to humiliate him. Jack stood in the middle of the street, ass naked holding his bloody face as he was forced to watch Kaine hop in his Benz and pull recklessly out into traffic.

# ERIC

# 36

Eric sat in one of the suites in his hotel staring at the wall, when he had gotten a call from Chico asking to meet up. The initial call was Chico asking for Eric to come out to Columbia and meet with him, but Eric quickly refused and suggested that if Chico wanted meet that they do on his stomping grounds. Eric returned back home to a lonely hotel room, then called and texted Kelly over one hundred times only to get the same result – no answer. Eric missed Kelly deeply and just wanted to hear her voice. With so much going on, Eric didn't have time to go out looking for Kelly, so instead he had assigned a team of his most trusted men to go out and find her. With all that was going on, Eric had just got word on Mike's latest whereabouts. It hurt his heart to hear about how Mike had sold the family out. With Jimmy being locked up at the moment, it was Eric's duty to go and take out Mike. Murder and Pistol Pete had volunteered to take Mike out, but this was something that Eric had to do himself.

Eric stepped out of his hotel room and was immediately met by Pistol Pete and three of his best bodyguards.

"Where we headed, out to meet Chico?" Pistol Pete asked as the five men entered the Cadillac truck that awaited curbside.

"Nah I have to make a quick stop first," Eric said as he gave the driver the address. Pistol Pete could tell that something was wrong from Eric's whole demeanor. Something about him was just off. "You alright boss man?"

Eric replied with a simple head nod. He had just given the driver Mike's new address, so from here on out there was no turning back. Eric stared out the window with a sad look on his face. When the truck came to a stop, Eric took a deep breath and stepped out of the backseat. Pistol Pete quickly hopped out of the truck behind Eric.

"Nah I have to do this myself," Eric told him. He entered the building, walked up to the third floor, and then exited the staircase. Eric pulled his 9mm from its holster and attached the silencer onto the barrel as he slowly walked down the hall. Eric reached the door he was looking for, shot the lock off the door, and then used his shoulder to bust through the front door. Eric entered the apartment and saw Mike sitting in the living room on the couch with a relaxed look on his face.

"So they sent you huh?" Mike said in a calm tone, as he looked Eric in his eyes. Mike's eyes went down to the .357 that rested on the coffee table then back up to Eric.

"Don't even think about it," Eric warned with his gun aimed at Mike's face.

"I don't have any more fight left in me," Mike said with a defeated look on his face. Eric could tell that living multiple lives had really beat Mike down and taken a toll on him.

"Before I kill you, just tell me why you did it?" Eric said. "Why did you put pop in jail?"

"Fuck pop, he's a selfish asshole!" Mike snapped. "I told him I wanted out the game and he threatened to go to the media and tell all about my dealings with the Mason family," Mike explained. "All I asked was to get out and be left alone, but I guess that was too much to ask."

Eric held his arm steady as the business end of his gun was pointed directly in Mike's face. "You know the rules Mike, it's never personal, business is always business."

Mike shook his head and gave Eric a sad look. "What I did to Derrick wasn't business," he paused so he could look Eric in his eyes. "It was personal."

Warm tears ran down Eric's face as he wrapped his finger down on the trigger.

Mike looked up at Eric and smiled. "Do what you gotta do. I'm at peace with myself and I'm not hiding anymore. Whatever is going to happen is just going to happen," he leaned back comfortably on the couch. "I remember when you was a good kid, now look at you. You ever ask yourself 'how did I get like this'?" Mike asked. "The answer is Derrick. I watched him literally turn you into a monster. You were supposed to be the money man, the only one in the family with a squeaky-clean record, just in case shit hit the fan, we all knew that you'd come to our rescue," Mike shook his head. "Now look at you standing here pointing a gun in my face. If shit was to hit the fan today who's left to rescue the family now? Millie tried her hardest to keep you away from all this shit but as soon as she went to prison I knew it would only be a matter of time before that snake Derrick sank his claws into you, now look at you." Mike chuckled as he leaned over and grabbed the remote from off the couch and turned the volume on the TV to its capacity. "Let get this shit over with!"

Eric stood their holding the gun in a shaky hand when he went to squeeze the trigger something in him just wouldn't let him do it. He slowly lowered his gun and wiped his eyes dry. "Pack your shit and leave this city and never come back!"

Mike shook his head defiantly. "I'm not going nowhere. I told you already whatever gon happen just gon have to happen."

"I'm not fucking around Mike!" Eric yelled. "I swear to god you better be gone in a week because when I come back, I'm going to blow your fucking head off!" He barked. "You have seven days to get the fuck out of my city!" Eric turned and made his exit.

Downstairs, Eric slid in the backseat of the Cadillac with a straight face. "Take me to the spot so we can meet up with Chico," he ordered.

"Couldn't do it, could you?" Pistol Pete rested a friendly hand on Eric's shoulder.

"I gave him a week to disappear forever," Eric said in a tone barely above a whisper.

"What happens if he doesn't leave?"

"Then I'll send you over there to take him out because I'm not going to be able to do it," Eric admitted shamefully.

"I understand," Pistol Pete said as he rubbed Eric's back.

# CHICO

# 37

Chico stepped out of the limousine with a bad limp. His leg still hadn't fully healed from when the assassin had ran up in his mansion and shot him. Chico and his ten-man security team stood in the abandoned warehouse awaiting Eric's arrival. Each man, including Chico, were heavily strapped and prepared to go to war if need be. Chico had promised that this would be a peaceful sit down, but after the assassination of his only child, he wasn't thinking too clearly.

Twenty minutes later, six black Cadillac trucks pulled up back to back with loud music bumping. Pistol Pete Murder and the rest of the security detail stepped out first to make sure that there wasn't any funny business going down. Once Pistol Pete felt that everything was on the up and up, he signaled for Eric to join them. Eric stepped out the back of the truck dressed in an expensive, tailored, navy blue suit with a slim, navy blue tie.

"Nice to see you again," Eric held out his hand for a handshake. Chico looked at Eric's hand as if it had just been pulled out of a sewer and left him hanging.

"This war between me and you is far from over," Chico began. "I just don't want to lose any more of my love ones and I'm sure you feel the same way."

"Why the fuck am I here?" Eric asked in an aggravated tone.

"I'm here to offer you three million dollars!" Chico said surprising everyone in the warehouse.

"Well I'm sure you not going to just *give* me three million dollars," Eric said obviously. "What do you want in return?"

"I want the name and the whereabouts of that hitman you hired," Chico said with a straight face. "What he did to me and my family will not go unpunished."

"Sorry, but I can't do that," Eric replied quickly.

"Four million dollars!"

Eric thought about it for a second. If he took the four million, he would have gotten the three million back that he paid the Black Dragon for the job, plus an extra one million profit. "Sorry but I don't do business like that."

"Five million!" Chico said with a straight face. "Trust and believe me that I'm going to find out everything I need to know about that hitman so you may as well be smart and take this free five million and give up the information." Chico had his resources on how to find out where to find the hit man but he was hoping that Eric would make his job a lot easier.

"Sorry, no can do," Eric said. He didn't want to give up the Black Dragon's info just in case Chico went back on his word and he needed to hire him again. Plus Eric didn't do shady business and would feel real grimy if he was to set the Black Dragon up like that.

"Is that your final answer?" Chico asked.

Eric nodded his head yes.

"I guess you're not as smart as you look," Chico said with a straight face. "I'll be seeing you again soon," he turned and disappeared in the back of his limousine.

# RICO

## 38

Rico sat in the passenger seat of the white B.M.W, counting a large stack of money, while his right-hand man Benny sat behind the wheel, cruising aimlessly through the streets of Harlem. As Rico sat counting his money, he heard his cell phone ring. He glanced down at the caller ID and saw Jack's name flashing across the screen. Rico quickly hit the ignore button and went back to counting his money. He knew that Jack was calling him about the twenty bricks that he had given him on consignment, but Rico didn't answer because he never intended on paying Jack for the work in the first place.

"I don't know why you ain't let me kill that clown!" Kaine said from the backseat. Kaine, Rico, and Benny all grew up together and they had all been getting money for years. People around their old neighborhood called the trio, "Three the Hard Way" because every time you saw those three at the same time, trouble was sure to follow.

"That clown not even worth a bullet," Rico waved him off. "Biggest bozo I ever seen."

"Yeah getting that work from him was like taking candy from a baby," Benny agreed. The trio weren't drug dealers; their main hustle was robbery. They all lived for the thrill of taking from the fortunate. Rico had gathered a team of hustlers to work for the trio. Each time they robbed a drug dealer, they would usually get money and product back. The product would then be distributed to all the hustlers that Rico had lined up ready to move the work. Business had been so good that now the trio was making more money off the drugs they took from the drug dealers than the cash and jewelry.

"Can't believe that clown is associated with the Mason's," Kaine said from the backseat.

"He ain't no real Mason," Rico shot back. "I did time with Jimmy Mason before and he wasn't no sucker. The rest of the Mason family is pretty solid. That Jack Mason cat is probably a fraud trying to use the name for protection," he shrugged.

"From what I been hearing, the Mason family been going through some tough times right now," Kaine told Rico. "They weak right now. Half of their muscle is locked up and the other half got killed by a bunch of wild-ass Columbians."

"So what you trying to say?" Rico asked with a raised brow. He didn't have a problem with the

Mason family, but if they were in his way or interfering with his money, than they had to go – no questions asked.

"What I'm trying to say, is the streets are all ours now," Kaine said with a smile. "We sat back and waited long enough. It's our turn now.

"Fuck, it lets do it," Rico said. "Starting tomorrow, we'll open up shop on all the vacant blocks and start letting motherfuckers know we out here."

"We definitely going to have put fire to a few of these clowns out here to let them know we ain't fucking around out here," Kaine said with a grin on his face. Kaine was as violent as they came and lived to put in work. The sad part about it all was that he cared more about street credibility than he cared about the money. To Kaine, it was all about having your name buzzing.

"What we need to do now is find the block that makes the most money and take that shit over!" Rico said. "Matter of fact, make a left right here." He said then three blocks later, he told Benny to make another left.

Benny pulled over in the middle of the block and double-parked. "What we looking at?"

"I heard this block here be doing crazy numbers," Rico said. "We'll stake out this block for a week learn who's who and anything else we need to know then it's take over time.

Kaine looked out the dark tinted window at the Dominican men who pretended not to be doing anything, when in all reality they were slanging drugs out of the building and the corner bodega as if it was free lunch. "Yeah this should be fun."

# ERIC

# 39

Eric stepped out the passenger seat of his Benz and quickly walked into the building that he had been looking for with Pistol Pete close on his heels. He had just gotten word on where Kelly was supposedly hiding-out. Needless to say, Eric headed to the address as soon as possible.

He stepped off the elevator, approached the door that he had been looking for, and gave it a strong knock. Seconds later, an older looking white woman answered the door. At first, she seemed to be in a good mood, but once she saw who was standing on the other side of the door, her mood instantly changed.

"What do you want and what are you doing here?" The lady said with an attitude.

"Sorry to bother you Ms. Taylor. I just wanted to know if your daughter was here." Eric asked. He knew that Kelly's mother hated his guts, not just because he was black, but also because he was also a criminal.

"She wants nothing to do with you, so please don't ever come back here again!" Ms. Taylor snapped. She went to slam the door in Eric's face, but he quickly stuck his foot in the door before she could shut it.

"Can I please speak to her for a second? It's very urgent," Eric pressed.

"She's not here!" Ms. Taylor barked. "I shipped her out of town. She told me that her life was in danger because of you!" She yelled with her finger pointed at Eric. "You are not welcome around here and if you come back again, it's going to be trouble!" She warned.

"Do you have a number for her?" Eric asked.

"Are you deaf or something? Didn't I just tell you to stay away from her?" Ms. Taylor yelled. Before Eric could reply, he heard movement coming from inside the house, followed by a big-bellied white man come to the door.

"What the hell is going on out here?" Mr. Taylor growled as he moved his wife out of the way. The second he laid eyes on Eric, Mr. Taylor's face turned beet red. "Get the hell out of my hallway this very second!"

"Sir, I'm just looking for my wife," Eric said respectfully.

"You have ruined my daughter's life!" Mr. Taylor yelled. "I told her she should have never married a *nigger*!" He let that last word roll off his tongue. Before Eric could respond, Mr. Taylor cleared his throat and spat in Eric's face. Before Mr.

Taylor even realized what was going on, Eric had already punched him in his face three times. Pistol Pete then jumped in and grabbed the old white man, picked him up, and dumped him down violently on his head. Pistol Pete pulled out his gun aimed it at Mr. Taylor's head and pulled the trigger.

"Noooo!" Eric yelled as he quickly shoved Pistol Pete's wrist just in time, causing the bullet to lodge into the wall right next to Mr. Taylor's head. "Come on let's go!" Eric said as he and Pistol Pete rushed down the stairs. He knew that if Pistol Pete killed Mr. Taylor, then they would have to kill his wife as well and Eric didn't want to be the one responsible for taking Kelly's parents lives. With the direction that Eric's life was heading, there was only one person that he could talk to that he trusted and could give him some sound advice.

# MILLIE

# 40

Millie laid on her bunk staring up at the ceiling with a smile on her face. The warden may have been keeping Millie out of population, but she could care less. In twenty-eight days, she would be a free woman again and she couldn't wait. While in the box, a C.O. on Millie's payroll made sure she had a cell phone, pen, paper, and plenty of books to read. While in isolation, Millie had been spending her time wisely putting together her masterplan for when she returned to the streets. Millie sat up on her bed when she heard her cell crack open and a C.O. walked in.

"Mason, you have a visitor," the officer announced as she stood and waited for Millie to get ready so that she could escort her down to the visiting room.

Seven minutes later, Millie stepped foot in the visiting room and smiled when she saw Eric sitting at the table with a smile on his face. "Heeeeey baby!" Millie said in a loud excited tone as she hugged Eric tightly. Millie sat down and could instantly see that something was bothering her favorite son. "I know that look, what's wrong?"

Eric let out a long breath. "Everything," he began. "I ran into Mike the other day."

"Oh yeah?" Millie asked, trying to read Eric's body language. "How did that go?"

Eric looked down at the floor. "I couldn't do it ma, I just couldn't."

Millie placed her hand on top of Eric's. "It's okay son, you did the right thing. At the end of the day he is your brother."

"But he put pops in jail."

"Your father is an O.G. he'll be alright," Millie said quickly. "Don't worry about him. What you need to be focused on is the future. We need Mike and his resources."

Eric shook his head. "You don't get it he's out of the game, he's done he won't help even if we wanted him to."

"You let me worry about Mike," Millie said with a smile. "I'll be out in less than a month and I'll take care of everything," she said confidently. "So I heard you got Chico to call the hit off."

Eric nodded his head. "Yeah I got him to call the hit off, but now he's offering me five million dollars to give him the name and whereabouts of the hitman I hired."

"Who'd you hire?" Millie asked. She had to admit that Eric was doing a hell of a job running the family business he was actually doing better than she expected.

"Some hitter from out in Miami who calls himself the Black Dragon."

"I think of heard of him what part of Miami he in?"

"South beach."

"I'm proud of you and want you to know that you are doing a hell of a job keeping this family above water," Millie looked Eric in his eyes.

"I still have to find us a connect because Chico still won't sell to us," Eric said. "Small-time hustlers are beginning to take over our territory because we haven't had product in months."

"Listen son, don't worry about all that. I'll take care of everything when I get home. All I need you do is keep doing what you're doing," Millie told him. "I'm going to write Mike a letter and let him know that he's family and will always be family. What I need you to do is make sure that nothing happens to him. I'll talk to him when I get home and fix everything."

Eric smiled; his mother sure knew how to fix anything no matter how bad they were.

"So how has that wife of yours been treating you?" Millie asked. She couldn't stand Kelly's guts, but stayed respectful because of Eric.

Eric shook his head. "She left me after Chico put the hit on the family," he said shamefully.

"Fuck that bitch!" Millie spat. "You were too good for her anyway. You know what you need?"

"What?"

"You need a real woman in your life. Somebody nice, sexy, someone that's going to hold you down and be there no matter what."

"I don't even think they make girls like that no more," Eric chuckled. Lately he had been too busy to go out and search for a new woman.

"I got the perfect girl for you. Her name is Nicole. I'm going to call her to tonight and give her your number," Millie said. "I want you to go out with her and enjoy yourself."

"What she look like?"

"Trust me, you're going to love her," Millie said confidently. "She's beautiful and a really good woman. I met her while I was in here."

"So now you want me to go out with a convict," Eric joked.

"She's a good girl son; she just landed in here because of some scumbag guy she was dealing with. Cops pulled them over and found drugs in the car. Since the car was in her name, the cops arrested her instead of the guy," Millie explained. "The guy let her take the rap and left her for dead."

Eric looked down at his watch. "I have to get going. Tell your girl to call me, but if she's crazy, I ain't messing with her."

"Trust me, she'll keep you on your toes," Millie said with a devilish smile on her face as she stood up and hugged her son tightly then turned and made her exit.

When Millie made it back to her cell, the first thing she did was grab her cell phone. She dialed a few numbers and then placed the phone up to her ear. On the fourth ring, a man picked up. "Who's this?"

"This is Millie Mason. May I speak to Chico please?"

"What the hell do you want? I already called the hit off," Chico said with an attitude.

"I heard you were looking for the hitter that shot your little girl. I think I may can help you."

"Don't fuck with me Millie!" Chico barked and got extremely serious. "If you have some valuable information, give it to me."

"Five million and I'll give you his name and the city you can find him in. You'll have to do the rest on your own," Millie offered. "So do we have a deal or what?"

Chico took a long second to think about it. "Yes we have a deal."

"Great I'll let you know where to wire the money," Millie said then ended the call.

# RICO

# 41

"Last time I'm going to ask you. Where's the money?" Rico asked in a calm tone with his gun pointed at Peanut's head. Peanut was a drug dealer well known for showboating and boasting.

"I don't have no money man," Peanut lied as he heard Kaine tearing up his apartment searching for the stash. The money he had stashed away in his apartment was all the money to his name and he couldn't chance loosing that.

Rico turned his gun on the girl that laid next to Peanut. "Peanut don't make me do this, just tell us where the money is and we'll leave," he tried to reason with the man. Before Peanut could reply, Kaine emerged from the backroom, carrying a duffle bag and an angry look on his face.

"Motherfucker!" Kaine growled. "You made me search the whole apartment for $60,000?"

"I'm sorry I was just trying to..."

Blocka! Blocka! Blocka!

Kaine pumped three shots into the back of Peanut's head then turned his gun on Peanut's girlfriend and shot her in the face.

Blocka!

Rico looked at Kaine and shook his head. "That wasn't necessary."

"We have to let the streets know that we not fucking around," Kaine said. "Can't show no weakness in this business." Kaine was looking to install fear into the rival dealers. So when it was time to take over they wouldn't have problems. Rico and Kaine made it back downstairs and hopped in the awaiting stolen car. Benny sat behind the wheel and once he saw that his team was in the car safely he quickly pulled away from the curb.

"So how did go?" Benny asked keeping his eyes on the road. He could tell by the look on Rico's face that whatever had went down upstairs wasn't good.

"It went according to plan," Kaine answered quickly. "We letting all these motherfuckers know that there's a new sheriff in town, one block at a time."

"What we need to focus on now is finding a new connect," Rico said quickly changing the subject. "We have enough product to last us maybe two months."

"Well you and Benny can work on the connect, while I'm work on letting the streets know we ain't fucking around." Kaine said with a murderous look in his eyes.

For the rest of the ride, Rico remained quiet as he stared blankly out the window. He had never wanted to be a criminal, but unfortunately, the only thing he was good at was crime. He had tried to get a job and go the civilian route, but after working at his job for three days, he got fired for knocking out his supervisor. From that point on, Rico decided to just stick to what he knows best and that's the streets.

# ERIC

# 42

Eric followed the direction of the GPS and arrived in front of a beautiful apartment building. After all, Eric decided to take his mother's advice and give Nicole a call. He had no clue what Nicole looked like, but at the moment he needed a female to take his mind off of Kelly and figured going out on one date wouldn't hurt. Eric pulled out his phone and dialed Nicole's number. On the third ring, she picked up. "Hello?"

"Hey this is Eric. I'm downstairs."

"Sorry, but I'm running a little late. You are more than welcome to come upstairs. I should be ready in a minute," Nicole said in her best phone-sex operator voice. "Come on up. I'll leave the door open apartment 11B."

"I'll be up in a second," Eric ended the call, turned on his hazard lights. and stepped out of his Benz. He was dressed in an expensive burgundy suit. Parked behind the Benz was a Cadillac truck filled with armed security that was paid to protect Eric. Pistol Pete stepped out the passenger seat of the truck and escorted Eric inside the building.

"So what shorty look like?" Pistol Pete asked once the two were on the elevator.

Eric shrugged. "I don't know. This going to be my first time seeing her." He stepped off the elevator and headed down the hall until he found the door he was looking for. Eric had never been on a blind date in his life, so he had no clue what was waiting for him on the other side of the door. All he knew was that Millie said he would like her and if it was one person, he trusted, it was Millie. Eric grabbed the doorknob and let himself inside of the apartment. "Hello." He said out loud.

"I'll be out in a second!" Nicole yelled from the bathroom. "Make yourself at home!"

Eric looked around and had to admit that Nicole's apartment was nice, and looked as though it was expensive. He helped himself to a seat on the couch and began checking his emails off of his phone.

Nicole stepped out of the bathroom and cleared her throat. "Well hello handsome," she smiled. Nicole stood 5'8 with full lips, wide hips, and sexy, toned legs. In the face, she looked just like the actress, Sanaa Lathan.

Eric quickly stood to his feet with a huge smile on his face. "Hey Nicole, it's nice to meet you," he extended his hand.

"We give hugs over here," Nicole said, evading Eric's personal space and wrapping her arms around his muscular back. Eric felt Nicole press her titties up against his chest as he inhaled her fragrance.

"Damn you smell good."

"Good enough to eat I hope," Nicole bit down on her bottom lip, openly flirting.

When Eric and Nicole stepped out into the hallway, Pistol Pete had to take a double take. He wasn't expecting Nicole to look as good as she did.

"This here is my bodyguard and friend, Pistol Pete." Eric introduced him.

"Nice to meet you Pete, I'm Nicole," she extended her hand only to have Pistol Pete kiss it gently.

"Pleasure is all mine," Pistol Pete said with a smile.

Outside, Eric and Nicole got inside the Benz and pulled out into the street with the Cadillac truck in their rear view mirror.

"So," Nicole smiled. "Your mother told you were a very important man."

"Yeah sorry about all the security, but it's better to be safe than sorry," Eric said.

"It's okay I don't mind, plus I already know what kind of business you and your mother are into," Nicole said as she openly checked out Eric's package. "Your mom took me under her wing while I was in jail. I owe her my life,"

"Yeah Millie is a good woman."

"I have good skills but while I was in there she really taught me a better way to put them to use and capitalize off of them," Nicole said.

"I'm glad to hear that," Eric said keeping his eyes on the road.

"So what's the plan for tonight?" Nicole asked excitedly.

"Whatever you wanna do," Eric shrugged. "I'm down for whatever."

"Hungry?"

"I could use a bite."

"Great, I heard about this new Jamaican restaurant that's supposed to be popping. Wanna go check it out?" Nicole asked.

"Sure," Eric answered. He didn't really care where they went. He was just happy to be spending time with Nicole. She was beautiful, funny, and down to earth, not to mention she had an ass like Serena Williams, which Eric loved. Eric pulled up in front of the Jamaican restaurant and immediately felt a bad vibe when he saw three Jamaican men standing posted up in front of the restaurant.

"I heard the food here is great," Nicole smiled as she stepped out of the Benz. She wore an all-black sundress that clung perfectly to her body and really showed off her curves well. On her feet were a pair of four inch heels that costed $500, her hair hung freely, stopping just short of her mid-back. Nicole immediately grabbed Eric's hand when she felt how the Jamaican men were openly checking her out.

"Bum-ba-clot!" One of the Jamaican men said loudly when Nicole walked pass. The remark caused Eric to stop dead in his tracks.

"Fuck you just said?" Eric said heading in the direction of the three men. He knew Nicole wasn't his girl, but she could have been.

"Me nah talk eh to you pussy boy," the Jamaican said with a heavy accent as his hand slipped down to his waistline. Before the Jamaican knew what was going on, Pistol Pete and several other of Eric's bodyguards had their guns trained on him.

"Apologize to my lady," Eric said standing nose to nose with the Jamaican man.

"Me sorry," The Jamaican flashed a yellow tooth smile. "Me no mean no harm."

"Come on baby, let's go eat," Nicole grabbed Eric's arm and pulled him towards the entrance. "Don't pay those clowns no mind."

Eric sat down at the table with a frown on his face. He couldn't believe the audacity of the Jamaican men that stood out front. Sitting at the table across from Eric and Nicole were Pistol Pete and another one of his bodyguards.

"Calm down Eric, don't let them get ruin your night," Nicole said as she heard her cell phone ringing. She removed her phone from her pocketbook and saw Millie's name flashing across the screen. "It's your mom," she said as she answered. "Hey girl."

"Did you take care of that for me yet?" Millie asked.

"Not yet we just got here," Nicole smiled.

"Aight cool. Text me when it's done and don't forget don't let Eric know what's going on," Millie reminded her.

"Yes of course, I'll let you know how the food is," Nicole said then ended the call so Eric wouldn't get suspicious.

"She still checking up on me like I'm a kid," Eric laughed.

"There goes that pretty smile," Nicole reached out and pinched his cheek like a baby.

"I'm sorry, but if you don't mind, I'd like to go somewhere else and eat," Eric said. "These fucking Jamaicans done really pissed me off."

"Sure no problem. I just need to run to the little girl's room real quick," Nicole grabbed her oversized pocketbook and headed towards the back of the restaurant. Nicole reached the restroom, but instead of going inside, she made a detour towards the door that said employees only. Nicole walked through the door and was immediately stopped by a rough looking Jamaican.

"Hey you no come back here!" The Jamaican barked as he started towards Nicole. Nicole slipped her hand down inside her purse and when she removed her hand, a four-inch blade was in it. Before the Jamaican knew what was going on, Nicole quickly slid the blade across the man's throat, and dropped her pocketbook. Before Nicole's pocketbook hit the floor, she had already removed her silenced .380 from her thigh holster and put a bullet right between the Jamaican man's eyes. The sound of the Jamaican man's body hitting the floor grabbed the attention of two other Jamaicans. The two Jamaican men rounded the corner and Nicole quickly put them both down with headshots.

Pst! Pst!

Nicole eased her way down the hall, when another Jamaican man surprised her and knocked her gun out of her. The man grabbed Nicole by the throat and roughly forced her back into the wall. He went to punch Nicole in the face, but she weaved the punch just in time causing the man's fist to lodge in the wall. Nicole grabbed the man's arm and hit it upward, snapping it at the elbow; with the same hand, she landed a crushing elbow to the man's rib cage before she hip tossed him down to the floor. Nicole took the man down so fast that it looked like a scene in a Kung-Fu movie. Nicole looked up and saw another Jamaican man emerge from around the corner with a machete in his hand. Before the man got a chance to swing the machete, Nicole had already kicked him in his face three times with the same leg. She then finished him off with a spinning wheel kick to the side of the head. Nicole watched as the man's head violently bounced off the floor. She quickly walked over, grabbed her gun off the floor along with her pocket, and headed to the back door. Nicole raised her gun and shot the lock off the back door then kicked it open. She stepped inside the back room and saw a Jamaican man sitting at a table covered in cash with a scared look on his face. "Please don't shoot I'm just..."

Pst!

Nicole quickly silenced the man with a bullet to the face. She then placed her gun back in her thigh holster. Nicole quickly stuffed her oversized pocketbook with as much cash as it could hold.

Nicole walked from the back as if she hadn't just killed six men. "You ready?" She asked Eric with a smile.

"Was waiting on you," Eric said as the two exited the restaurant. When Nicole got back in the car, she made sure that she sat her pocketbook in the back seat. Nicole put her seat belt on and quickly wiped a few dots of blood off of her arm. "I hope those guys didn't ruin your night."

"I'm good," Eric said with a fake smile on his face. The truth was that Eric wanted to go back in the restaurant and kill every last one of the Jamaicans who had disrespected him. The only reason things didn't hit the fan tonight was because

Eric didn't want to scare Nicole with an act of violence on their first night out, but little did he know that Nicole was as violent as they came. Eric pulled up in front of Nicole's building and placed the gear in park. "Sorry about dinner."

"It's okay, I understand," Nicole brushed it off. She grabbed Eric's hand and looked him in his eyes. "You have been the perfect gentleman and thank you for taking me out tonight. I'm sure our next date will be amazing."

Eric leaned over and kissed Nicole passionately. "Thank you for tonight. It was a pleasure meeting you and would love to do this again.

Nicole smiled. "Anytime," she leaned over and kissed him on the lips. Nicole stepped out the car, opened the backdoor and grabbed her pocketbook, and then disappeared inside of her building. When Nicole made it back inside of her apartment and quickly removed her gun from her thigh holster and sat it down on the counter. Nicole was glad that she was able to do the job without raising any suspicion with Eric because that would of surely ruined everything.

# RICO

# 43

Rico stepped out the bedroom with a cool bop dressed in all black. Tonight, he and his crew were heading to a club to get their faces out there and let the streets know that they were here to stay. Rico was against having his face in the lime light, but felt as if he had to support his team. All Rico cared about was getting paid and taking care of his family. He had been to jail twice and vowed that he would rather die than step foot in another jail. Rico stepped in the living room and saw his eight-month pregnant girlfriend Samantha laying on the couch.

"Hey baby, where you going?" Samantha asked looking up at the clock that hung on the wall that read 10:30 p.m.

"Me and the team going to hit up the club tonight," Rico said as he leaned down and kissed, Samantha's pregnant belly.

"Please be careful Rico, the last thing we need is for you to end up back in jail," Samantha said with a worried look on her face. The last two times Rico went to jail, Samantha held him down the entire time, and the time away from her man killed her.

"Baby I told you a hundred times that I'm never going back to jail," Rico told her.

"I hate when you go out with that asshole Kaine," Samantha huffed. She couldn't stand Kaine. In her eyes, he was just trouble waiting to happen. Every time Kaine came around, it just made Samantha's skin crawl.

"I know baby, but I promise I won't be out too late tonight," Rico lied. He knew with Samantha being pregnant she didn't need to be stressing herself out over nonsense.

"I love you baby, be careful," Samantha kissed Rico on the lips then watched him walk out the door.

\*\*\*

Rico arrived to the club and met up with Benny and Kaine in the parking lot. Rico took one look at Kaine and could see that he was already drunk, which was a bad sign. A sober Kaine was bad, but a drunk Kaine was ten times worst and right now, Rico wanted to get through the night without incident. "You good?"

"I'm great," Kaine flashed a drunken smile as he openly checked out a pack of chicks walking by. "Damn!" He snarled as he checked out all of their asses. "Come on, all the hoes are inside," he said as the trio headed towards the entrance.

# JACK MASON

## 44

Jack sat in the passenger seat of his pearl white Benz, staring out the window at all the beautiful women that stood on the long line to get inside the club. Jack stepped out onto the sidewalk dressed in an expensive looking black suit. Alongside Jack were three of his best bodyguards. He decided to beef up his security after getting robbed in broad daylight. Jack and his crew were escorted straight inside the club and led straight to the table they had reserved. As Jack walked through the club, he spotted the man that had robbed and humiliated him sitting over at his own table with a bottle in his hand. Jack quickly headed over into Kaine's direction. There was no way he could let Kaine get away with what he did to him like that. When Jack got within striking range, he pulled his 9mm from his holster and let it rip.

Blocka! Blocka! Blocka! Blocka! Blocka!

Jack let off five rounds and then quickly blended in with the rest of the crowd that scrambled to get out of the club without getting shot.

\*\*\*

Rico sat in the cut sipping on his drink when he heard a loud series of gunshots ring out. Things happened so fast that before he could figure out what was going on, he saw Benny laid out on the floor with two holes in his chest. "Shit!" Rico cursed as he kneeled down next to Benny's body. He looked up, saw Kaine hop over the rail down into the crowd, and began returning fire.

Kaine pushed his way through the crowd in search of his target. He was so drunk that he didn't spot Jack until after the shots had rang out. Kaine aimed his gun in Jack's direction and fired off four shots in rapid succession.

\*\*\*

Jack rushed through the club as innocent party goers dropped left and right next to him. Jack spilled out the front door, quickly climbed in the driver's seat of the Benz, and pulled off in a hurry, leaving his security behind. Jack drove down the highway with a smile on his face. He may not have shot Kaine, but shooting a member of his squad was just as refreshing. Thirty minutes later, Jack stepped inside his baby mansion feeling good about himself. He walked to the refrigerator, grabbed a beer, and then headed upstairs to the master bedroom. Jack removed his suit jacket and took a sip of his beer when he saw a figure dressed in all black emerge from his bathroom. "What the fuck?" Jack said with a confused look on his face. "Who the hell are you?"

Nicole stood before him dressed in all black with a silenced 9mm aimed at his head. "Millie said to tell you goodnight," Nicole pulled the trigger and exited the room before Jack's body hit the floor. Out in the hallway stood one of Jack's bodyguards. Nicole crept up behind the guard and slit his throat from ear to ear. Downstairs, Nicole ran into another guard she quickly put him down with a silenced bullet to the back of the head.

Pst!

Nicole stepped over the guard's body when another guard walked in on her. Nicole quickly put the big man down with two quick shots to the chest, but before the guard went down, he managed to get one shot off. That one shot was all it took to alert all the other guard's that something was wrong.

"Shit," Nicole cursed as she scrambled towards the exit. She ran around the corner and was roughly tackled down to the floor by a three hundred pound guard. Nicole grabbed the big man's arm, swirled underneath him, and somehow got the big man's arm into an arm bar.

"Urggggghhh!" The big man howled as he heard his bone snap. Nicole made it back to her feet just in time to see two more guards rush inside the room. Nicole quickly grabbed two throwing knives from her utility belt and tossed them at the two guards. Both guards grabbed their throats then went down. Nicole stepped outside, put down three more guards with her perfect aim, and then disappeared in the bushes.

# SAMANTHA

# 45

Samantha laid on the couch in a daze as the TV watched her. She was supposed to be in the house resting, but instead she was stressing. Samantha would never be able to rest properly while Rico was out running the streets. It seemed like the harder she tried to rest, the more her mind wondered. Samantha stood up and walked to the kitchen to get a bottle of water. She trusted Rico, but she just hated when he was out with Kaine. The problem she had with Kaine was that he didn't think, he just did things and just from meeting him only a few times, Samantha could tell that Kaine didn't care about his life and didn't mind sitting in jail for the rest of his life. She never understood how Rico could be friends with someone like that. Samantha waddled back over towards the couch when she heard the front door open and Rico stepped inside with blood on his shirt.

"Oh my god!" Samantha stood to her feet and placed her hand over her mouth.

"It's not my blood," Rico said quickly as he closed the door behind him.

"Are you okay? What happened?" Samantha fired off questions back to back with a worried and scared look on her face. This was just why she hated when Rico hung out with Kaine.

"Was at the club and things got a little crazy," Rico said with a shrug. He was hoping that Samantha would be sleep when he got in but he had no such luck.

"Rico, what happened?" Samantha asked with her hands on her hips. "And don't give me no bullshit!"

Rico huffed. "Was at the club and some guy that Kaine had static with showed up and started dumping shots," he gave her the short version.

"How did I know that Kaine had something to do with this?" Samantha spat. "He's going to get you killed!"

"I don't wanna hear this shit tonight," Rico headed down the hall until Samantha firmly grabbed his wrist stopping his motion.

"I'm leaving!" Samantha snapped. "I can't sit around and watch you throw your life away like this."

Rico grabbed Samantha and stopped her from heading down the hall. "Fuck you mean you leaving? I thought we was in this together I'm doing this for us!"

"You not doing this for us. You doing this for yourself!" Samantha snapped. "I don't need or care about none of this shit!"

"Baby I'm just trying to give us a better life that's all," Rico said.

"What good is having everything, if you in jail and you can't even enjoy it?" Samantha barked. "You smarter than that Rico. Please start using your head. We can't live how we used to live and we can't take the risks that we used to take because we have a family now," Samantha looked down at her swollen stomach.

"I promise from now on I'll make sure I move smarter," Rico promised. "And as soon as the baby gets here I'm done."

Samantha's face lit up. "Say that's your word."

"That's my word baby," Rico pulled, Samantha in and hugged her tight. "I love you baby."

"I love you more."

# NICOLE

## 46

Nicole stepped out of her drop top Benz and handed her keys to the valet that stood out front. She walked inside the five-star hotel looking like a million bucks. She was dressed in a nice form fitting black gown that came down to her ankles, a beautiful necklace glittered around her neck, and the bracelet on her wrist stood out even more. The brunette wig and dark sunglasses gave Nicole a little more swagger in her walk as she approached the front desk and smiled at the man behind the counter. She reached inside her purse and slid the man an envelope filled with cash.

The clerk quickly took the envelope and in return, he slid Nicole a room key. "Room 505," he whispered.

Nicole took the key and headed for the elevators. She stepped on and pressed five. Nicole made sure she kept her head down so the camera couldn't capture her image. Nicole stepped off the elevator and headed towards room 505. Nicole looked over both shoulders before she swiped the card key across the lock and let herself into the room. Nicole walked inside the room and saw a white chick laying across the bed asleep. "Wake the fuck up!" She yelled causing the white girl to jump up with a startled look on her face.

"What are you doing in my room?" The white girl asked with fear in her eyes.

"Is your name Kelly Mason?" Nicole asked as she removed a photo from her purse to confirm she was looking at the right girl.

"What do you want from me?" Kelly asked with a scared look on her face.

"Millie Mason sent me here to kill you," Nicole said as she removed her .380 with the silencer attached from her thigh holster. "So you're Eric's wife," Nicole said with a look on her face that said she wasn't impressed.

"You know my husband?" Kelly asked. "Can I please call him real quick?"

"Eric's my man now and he doesn't need any distractions," Nicole said as she raised her arm aiming her gun at Kelly's head and pulled the trigger.

Pst!

Nicole placed her gun back in her thigh holster when the room door opened and another woman stepped inside.

"Who the hell are you?" The woman asked with a confused look on her face. Nicole walked up to the girl with a smile on her face and as soon as she got within striking distance, she made her move. Nicole watched as the girl's head violently snapped back as her jab landed in the center of her face. Nicole quickly swept the girl's legs from under her, pinned her down with her knee on her chest, and wrapped her hands around the girl's neck. Nicole watched as the girl's face turned bright red and her legs kicked and moved as she tried to remove the death grip that Nicole had around her throat. The girl desperately clawed at Nicole's arm but it was no use, Nicole's grip was too strong. Two minutes later, the girl's body finally stopped moving. Nicole stood to her feet, fixed her dress, and then exited the room as if nothing happened.

Downstairs, Nicole got back in her rented drop top Benz and pulled away from the hotel in a hurry. On the ride back to the airport, Nicole thought about Eric. Even though she hadn't known him that long, she had to admit that she was definitely feeling him and could see herself with a man like him. Nicole may have liked Eric, but she still worked for Millie.

Nicole returned the rental, ditched all her weapons, and then took the shuttlebus to the airport. Nicole walked through the airport. She heard her cell phone ring, looked down at the screen, and smiled when she saw Eric's name pop up on her screen. "I was just thinking about you," she answered.

"I was thinking about you too," Eric sang. "I miss you and want to see you."

Nicole looked down at her watch. "I have a few things to do meet me at my place in about five hours?"

"That's perfect. I have a couple of things I need to handle as well," Eric said. "So five hours will be good."

"Aight bae I'll hit you in a minute," Nicole said then ended the call. As Nicole walked through the terminal, she noticed two white men following her. They had been following her ever since she entered the airport. St first, she thought they were cops, but from the way they carried themselves she knew right away that they definitely weren't cops. Nicole walked regular then quickly stepped inside the ladies room.

\*\*\*

"Don't let that bitch out of your site," Eddie said. He and his brother Marcus had been trying to track Nicole down for the past five years. Five years ago, Nicole had murdered their mother in cold blood. When Eddie and Marcus came home that night, they saw Nicole running away from their home. From that point on, they vowed to find the woman that murdered their mother and kill her. The only problem was they had to get rid of their weapons upon entering the airport. Weapons or no weapon, they were going to make the woman who murdered their mother pay.

"I'm on her," Marcus said with a serious intense look on his face. "She just went in the ladies room."

"This is the perfect opportunity," Eddie said as he headed towards the ladies room and quickly stepped inside. Marcus was the last one in the restroom and he quickly locked the door behind him. From first glance, the restroom appeared to be empty, but Eddie knew better. He bent down, peeked under all the stalls, and didn't see any feet. Eddie walked up to the first stall and kicked the door open.

Bang!

Empty.

Eddie walk up to the next stall and kicked the door open.

Bang!

Empty.

He reached the third door and before he could raise his leg to kick the door open, the door opened on its own and Nicole rushed out and tackled Eddie back into the sink. Nicole grabbed Eddie's head and slammed it into the mirror shattering it. Nicole went to punch Eddie in his face when she saw Marcus creeping up on her out of the corner of her eye. She quickly delivered a sidekick that landed on Marcus's chin. The kicked dazed him a bit but didn't drop him.

In that split second, Eddie grabbed Nicole in a bear hug and tried to squeeze the life out of her.

"Urggh!" Nicole groaned as she felt her oxygen begin to cut off. She quickly landed a crushing head-butt that shattered Eddie's nose. The pain was so severe that he was forced to take a knee. Nicole used that opportunity to slip behind Eddie and put him in a chokehold. Before Eddie could get his second wind, Nicole gave his neck a hard twist until she heard a loud popping sound. Nicole stood to her feet and faced Marcus. Marcus charged Nicole, grabbed her as he hit her hard lifting her up off her feet, and drove her into the hard, unforgiving wall. Nicole hit Marcus with a rabbit punch, a shock to his temple that stunned him. Nicole quickly grabbed Marcus's shirt, spun him around, and slammed his head into the tiled wall. Marcus tried to fight back but a vicious knee to the pit of his stomach stopped all that. The pain was so bad that Marcus doubled over in pain and dropped down to his knees. "I'm sorry please don't kill me," he begged as tears of fear rolled down his face.

"Who sent you?" Nicole asked breathing heavily as she stood over Marcus.

"Nobody sent us. Me and my brother had been following you for years," Marcus explained. "You killed our mother five years ago."

Nicole had killed so many people in the past few years it was impossible for her to try and figure out who their mother was. "Stop crying and get your punk-ass up!" Nicole snatched Marcus to his feet, slipped behind him, and put him in a deadly chokehold. Nicole applied tight pressure as she heard Marcus struggle to get air. Nicole dropped down to the floor and wrapped her legs around Marcus's waist applying even more pressure to the chokehold. Nicole kept Marcus in the chokehold until he finally stopped moving. She picked herself up off the floor and quickly exited the bathroom and blended in with the rest of the crowd in the terminal.

# THE BLACK DRAGON

# 47

The Black Dragon laid on the floor of his living room with his feet shoved under the couch doing sit-ups. In his line of work, he had to be prepared for anything so he made sure he always took care of his body by staying in tiptop shape. The Black Dragon loved his job and was always ready for anything. The Black Dragon's motto was that it was better to stay ready so that he didn't have to get ready. The Black Dragon got into push-up form when he looked up at his laptop screen, which he used as his surveillance, and saw an army of Columbian looking men creeping down his hallway holding assault rifles in their hands.

The Black Dragon quickly hopped up off the floor, only having time to grab his FiveSeven handgun from off the couch before his front door was blown off the hinges. The Black Dragon dropped the first three gunmen that were brave enough to come running through the front door. He then took cover behind the wall as several different guns could be heard being fired all at the same time. The Black Dragon stuck his arm around the corner and fired blindly out into the crowd. From the loud grunts and the sound of bodies hitting the floor, he knew that he had hit his targets. Before the Black Dragon could think of his next move, a brave gunman ran around the corner. Aimlessly, the Black Dragon grabbed the nose of the man's rifle and shot him in the back. He quickly stuck his handgun down in the small of his back, spun around the corner with his finger pressed down on the trigger, and bullet shells popped out of the side of the machine gun continuously, as gunmen dropped left and right.

Just when the Black Dragon thought he had took all of the gunmen out, he saw an arm toss two grenades inside his apartment. "Shit!" The Black Dragon yelled as he took off in a sprint and threw himself through the glass window just as the grenades exploded.

Booooooooom!

Fifteen seconds later, the gunman that tossed the grenades inside the apartment slowly eased his way inside. He searched the entire apartment and saw no sign of the assassin. The gunman slowly made his way over to the window and peeked out, when out of nowhere, a hand shot up and snatched him out the window. The Black Dragon lifted himself up with one hand and shot the last four remaining gunmen in rapid succession with the other hand.

Boc! Boc! Boc! Boc!

The Black Dragon pulled himself back inside his apartment with a grunt and just laid on the floor for a second and tried to gather his thoughts. His forehead and arms were all cut up from him jumping through the window. He looked down and saw a bullet hole in his shoulder. "Fuck!" The Black Dragon cursed as he picked himself up off the floor and quickly made his exit before the cops showed up.

# ERIC

# 48

"**F**or a second, I thought you weren't going to show up," Nicole stepped to the side so that Eric could enter her apartment.

The first thing Eric noticed was that Nicole had answered the door dressed in a pair of fishnet stockings and a matching red bra and thong set. "I wouldn't of missed this for the world," Eric said as he moved in and cuffed Nicole's ass while the two shared a long drawn-out, sloppy kiss.

"I need to feel you," Nicole moaned in Eric's ear as she placed a few wet kisses on his neck. Eric unsnapped Nicole's bra, carried her over to the couch where he pulled her thong to the side, and slowly licked in between her thighs.

"Mmmm!" Nicole moaned loudly as she enjoyed Eric's mouth. Eric's tongue made circles, as he sucked on her clit, licked figure eights, gave her the sweetest torture known to women. Eric's mouth made loud slurping noises, as he tasted her sweet juices. Nicole jerked and moaned as if the devil inside her was fighting for freedom, and then suddenly, her legs clamped down around Eric's head as her body began to tremble. Eric watched her. Felt her. Enjoyed her orgasm as much as she did.

"Get over here you animal!" Nicole growled through clenched teeth as she roughly tossed Eric down on the couch, mounted him, and slipped his rod inside of her warm soaking wet box. "Sssss," Nicole hissed as she slowly bounced up and down on Eric. "Oh my god this dick is so good!" She grabbed the sides of Eric's face and shoved her tongue down his throat. Once Nicole got used to Eric's size, she planted her feet down on the couch and began to bounce up and down on his dick like a mad woman. Nicole held on to Eric as he began to thrust upwards. Nicole dug her nails into Eric's skin, bit down on her bottom lip, trying to swallow her rising moans. Nicole closed her eyes and made ugly faces as she felt Eric's length sliding in and out of her. "Oh shit!" He groaned as he quickly pulled himself out of Nicole's warm box and exploded all over his stomach and torso.

"Oh my god you are a monster," Nicole smiled devilishly as she looked down at Eric's package one last time before she went to the bathroom to get a wet soapy washcloth. Eric laid back on the couch when he heard his cell phone ring. Too tired to move, he just allowed it to ring out. Nicole returned from the bathroom and began cleaning Eric off when his cell phone rang once again. "Pass me my phone please," Eric sat up. He looked down at the screen and saw that whoever was calling him was calling from a blocked number. "Yo who this?"

"You gave me up you sneaky motherfucker!" The caller barked into the phone.

Immediately Eric recognized that the voice on the other end of the phone belonged to the Black Dragon. "Huh what are you talking about?"

"You gave me up to Chico and told him where his men could find me," The Black Dragon yelled. "You fucked up big time!"

"I have no idea what you're talking about," Eric said truthfully. "Now start from the beginning and tell me what happen."

"All you need to know is that the Black Dragon is coming for you."

Eric looked down at his phone and saw that he had been hung up on.

"Is everything okay baby?" Nicole asked with a concerned look on her face.

"Yes baby I'm fine," Eric lied. "Everything is just fine."

# JIMMY

# 49

"Heeeeey baby," Cherokee ran and jumped in Jimmy's arms as he stepped foot out of the jailhouse. Jimmy cuffed Cherokee's ass firmly as the two shared a long drawn out kiss. If one didn't know any better you would think that Jimmy was just coming home from a ten-year sentence.

"Damn you smell good," Jimmy said placing Cherokee back down on her feet. He and Cherokee slid in the backseat as at the Range Rover pulled off. "I have to go see Eric, take me over to his spot real quick," Jimmy ordered from the backseat. For the entire ride, Cherokee couldn't keep her hands or her mouth off of him. She was so happy to see him it was crazy. Cherokee knew that Jimmy had only been gone for a few days but it didn't matter she still missed him like crazy. "You going to be a long time at Eric's house? I wanna give you something," Cherokee whispered in Jimmy's ear as she sucked on the bottom of his ear lobe.

"Nah I shouldn't be too long," Jimmy lied. He had to get up with Eric and get back in the loop on what was going on. The Range Rover pulled up in front of Eric's hotel. "I'll be back in a second baby," Jimmy leaned over and kissed Cherokee on the lips.

"Don't have me waiting too long daddy," Cherokee said with the sad puppy look on her face.

Jimmy stepped foot in the hotel and walked straight up to the counter skipping the long line of customers. "Hey, tell Eric that Jimmy's out here to see him," he said to the blonde hair woman that stood behind the counter. The blonde hair chick quickly picked up the phone on her desk and dialed a few numbers. She spoke in a hushed tone before hanging up. "Mr. Mason is in room 303," the blonde hair woman said with a friendly smile.

Jimmy stepped off the elevator and immediately spotted two security guards at the end of each hall. The guards acknowledged Jimmy with a simple head nod. He reached the door and gave it a strong knock. Seconds later, Pistol Pete answered the door and stepped to the side so Jimmy could enter. Jimmy stepped in the suite and saw Eric standing up over in the corner on an intense phone call.

"Say no more," Eric said ending his call. He looked up and smiled at Jimmy. "Welcome home," he said as he gave Jimmy dap followed by a hug.

"Did you take care of Mike yet?" Jimmy asked helping himself to a drink.

"Nah I spoke to Millie and she said she'll handle it," Eric replied. "She said we can still use him."

"Still use him?" Jimmy echoed with his face crumbled up. "He turned on the entire family he has to go point blank, period!"

"Millie will be home before the week is out," Eric shrugged. "We'll see how she handles this."

"Fuck this waiting around shit!" Jimmy huffed. "I'm going to take care of this shit tonight!"

"You can't do that," Eric said quickly. "I already gave Millie my word that we wouldn't make a move on this situation until she got home," with Millie coming home in the next few days, that would definitely take a lot of pressure up off of Eric and he couldn't wait to have his mother back by his side.

"What's Millie's plan?" Jimmy asked taking a sip from his drink.

Eric shrugged, "I have no idea," he answered honestly.

"I hope jail ain't turn her soft," Jimmy said. "What's up with Chico? I heard the hit has been taken off."

"Yeah I took care of that," Eric said with a smile. "All we need now is a new connect and we'll be good."

"It's this cat out in Florida. I heard he supposed to have the best quality stuff want me to go check him out?" Jimmy asked.

"Nah Millie said she already got that taken care of," Eric told him as he heard a loud knock at the door. Pistol Pete answered the door and saw one of the guards that was posted up out in the hallway at the door.

"What's up?" Pistol Pete asked.

"There's a few men downstairs asking for Eric," the guard informed him.

"Tell them I'll be down in a second," Eric said as he grabbed his gun off of the dresser and stuck it down in his holster.

Eric and his entourage made it downstairs and saw a mob of Italian men in nice suits standing over to the side. "How can I help you gentlemen?" Eric asked politely with a smile on his face.

The leader of the group quickly spoke up, "How you doing? My name is Frankie and there's a few things I need to speak to you about."

"Well my time is very valuable, so if you could get on with it," Eric said.

"Well you see, it's like this," Frankie began. "This hotel used to belong to a Mr. Chambers and Mr. Chambers works for my father. My father is the one to put up the capital for this hotel Mr. Chambers was just running the place for him. So you see Mr. Chambers was in no position to sign this place over to you." He explained.

"I hear what you saying but I think that's a problem that your father needs to take up with Mr. Chambers," Eric said in an even tone.

Frankie chuckled. "I'm afraid you don't understand this is my father's hotel and he wants it back."

"Who's your father?"

"Alex Russo," Frankie said proudly.

Eric had heard about the Russo family. They were supposed to be one of the last mob families left standing and known to have a violent by any means necessary history. "Listen, I wish I could help you out but I can't. Mr. Chambers signed the hotel over to me so whatever problems you have I suggest you take them up with him."

"I spoke to Mr. Chambers and he told me just how you got him to sign those papers," Frankie said with a scowl on his face. "I strongly urge you to sign this hotel back over to my father before things take a turn for the worst. We know all about the Mason family and their sneaky way."

"Gentlemen I really wish I could help you, but I have somewhere to be. Good day gentlemen," Eric said in a friendly tone with a smile on his face.

"Okay have it your way," Frankie said with an evil smirk on his face as him and his team of men exited the hotel. Right then and there, Eric knew that the, Russo family was going to be a problem and right now another problem was the last thing he needed.

"I think I did time with a member of the Russo family," Jimmy said. "They not to be fucked with."

"Yeah, so I've heard," Eric said, as he watched, Frankie and his crew make their exit.

# MILLIE

## 50

Millie stepped foot out of the jail with a huge smile on her face. She had finally been released, fifteen years behind bars and now finally she was a free woman. For a second, the moment didn't even feel real. It felt as if Millie was dreaming and living a fantasy. Millie took a deep breath and inhaled the fresh air. Millie took her time and walked down the path to the B.M.W that waited curbside for her. Millie was dressed in a pair of tight black jeans that looked as if they were glued on with a black blouse to match. On her feet were a pair of all black red bottoms, her hair was pulled back into a regular ponytail, and even without any make on she was still as pretty as they came. Millie favored the singer Ashanti. Millie grabbed the door handle and made herself comfortable in the passenger seat.

"Welcome home!" Nicole said excitedly behind the wheel of the B.M.W.

Millie flashed a smile. "It feels good to be back," she said honestly. "Now hurry up and get me the fuck away from this filthy-ass jail." Millie wanted to be as far away from the jail as possible. For the last fifteen years, prison was where she called home and now today, Millie could finally say that she was really going home.

Nicole pulled away from the curb like a mad woman. "So where to first?" She had to admit that she was happy to finally have her mentor home.

"I have to go see my son first."

"Who Eric?" Nicole asked keeping her eyes on the road.

"No, I have to go see Mike," Millie told her. "So did Chico wire my money over to you like he was supposed to?"

"Yup," Nicole smiled. "Five million dollars. I put it in the safe just like you told me to."

"What's good with them Jamaican niggaz you hit up over by the restaurant?" Millie asked as she reached into the back seat, grabbed the bottle of Peach Cîroc, cracked it open, and took a swig straight from the bottle.

"No sign of them. I already got a crew over in the old territory just like you told me to do," Nicole said proudly. "They had a nice little cash flow over there."

"What about Jack?"

"He's dead as a door knob," Nicole smiled. It felt good to be in a position of power for once and she could tell that Millie had the right formula to make them both multi-millionaires.

"Good I couldn't stand that motherfucker," Millie huffed. Just thinking about how grimy Jack was made her stomach turn. A part of her wished she could have been there to witness his death with her own eyes, but as long as he was dead that was all that matter. "You I know I wanted to kill Jack for years but I couldn't because he was Derrick's brother.

"That's what I'm here for," Nicole said with a smile. "Whatever you need me to do, just say the word."

"What about Kelly?" Millie asked.

"That one was my pleasure," Nicole said with an evil smirk on her face. In all reality, she would kill all of Eric's ex's if she could.

"You did a good job while I was gone," Millie praised Nicole. "In no time these streets will be mines again. What's up with you and Eric?"

"I threw this pussy on him real good just like you told me to," Nicole winked. "Pretty soon I'll have him eating out the palm of my hand."

"Good," Millie said as she opened the glove compartment and grabbed the .380 that sat inside and slipped it in her purse. "I told you Eric is sucker for women. His heart is too good for this business, so as long as you're controlling his thoughts we'll be good. I raised that boy I know all of his weaknesses. He doesn't know that you're a hit-woman does he?" Millie asked with a raised brow.

"Of course not."

Millie had heard about Nicole before she had met her in jail. It just happened to be luck that the two crossed one another's path. "I'm going to need you to watch my back while I'm out here cause I'm sure to make a lot if enemies."

"You know I always got your back," Nicole said as she pulled up in front of Mike's building. "So what's the plan for Mike?"

"He's my son," Millie answered quickly. "Now I have to go in there and fix this before he does any further damage to the family," she stepped out the car then disappeared inside the building. Just as her sons, Millie always took the stairs. The only time she took the elevator was when she was going up to the fifth floor or higher. Millie stepped out of the staircase, walked down the hall, and knocked on the door she was looking for. Seconds later, Mike answered the door with a huge smile on his face.

"Get in here!" Mike snatched Millie inside the apartment and hugged her tightly. "It's so good to have you back home!" Out of everyone in the Mason family, Millie was his favorite.

"Tell me about it," Millie smiled. "Now tell me what the hell is going on out here. I've heard so many different stories, now I need to hear what's going on straight from your mouth."

Mike sighed loudly. "After you left, things started getting real bad because of the decisions that pop was making," he walked over to the kitchen and poured him and Millie a drink. "Things had been bad for a while, plus on top of that, I had no time for my personal life. There I was doing all this work making all this money and I was miserable," Mike explained. "So I told Derrick that I wanted out and he threatened to tell the media about my involvement with the Mason family if I didn't cooperate," he looked down at the floor. "I know you and him adopted me when I was kid and took good care of me, but with all the work I've done for this family over the years, you would think he would be a bit understanding and reasonable. Not to mention he killed my girlfriend."

"You know how Derrick is, he doesn't mean any harm," Millie sipped her drink. "Listen this is what I need you to do. I need you back on my team. I need to know who all the major players are and I need to know if the F.E.D.S have anything on your brother Eric."

"Sorry mom but no can do," Mike said quickly. "I'm on vacation right now and I no longer work for the Mason family. No disrespect but, the Mason family can kiss my ass." He said aggressively.

Mike's last comment took Millie by surprise. "How dare you talk like that after all this family has done for you," Millie spat. "Me and Derrick took you off the streets and you repay him by putting him in jail for the rest of his life?"

Mike shrugged, "It was either him or me, and I'm going to choose me every time."

Millie stood to her feet and finished her drink. "Thanks for the drink son."

"No problem,"

"Damn I know you don't work for the Mason family anymore, but can your mother at least get a hug?" Millie said jokingly. Mike came forward and leaned in for a hug when Millie pulled her gun from her purse and shoved it up under Mike's chin and pulled the trigger, painting the ceiling with blood. Millie stood over Mike's dead body with a disgusted look on her face. "Punk motherfucker!" She growled as she fired three more shots into Mike's chest.

Blocka! Blocka! Blocka!

"I'm back home now!" Millie growled to know one in particular. "A lot of shit gon change around here!" She said as she fired one last shot into Mike's chest.

Blocka!


**TO BE CONTINUED...**

# Books by Good2Go Authors on Our Bookshelf

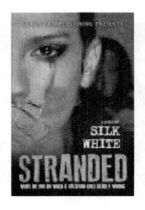

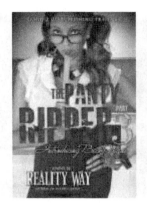

## Good 2 Go Films Presents

**THE HAND I WAS DEALT- FREE WEB SERIES**
**NOW AVAILABLE ON YOUTUBE!**

**YOUTUBE.COM/SILKWHITE212**

*To order books, please fill out the order form below:*

*To order films please go to www.good2gofilms.com*

Name:_____

Address:_____

City: _____ State: _____ Zip Code: _____

Phone:_____

Email:_____

Method of Payment:     Check     VISA     MASTERCARD

Credit Card#:_____

Name as it appears on card: _____

Signature: _____

| Item Name | Price | Qty | Amount |
|---|---|---|---|
| 48 Hours to Die – Silk White | $14.99 | | |
| Business Is Business – Silk White | $14.99 | | |
| Business Is Business 2 – Silk White | $14.99 | | |
| Flipping Numbers – Ernest Morris | $14.99 | | |
| Flipping Numbers 2 – Ernest Morris | $14.99 | | |
| He Loves Me, He Loves You Not - Mychea | $14.99 | | |
| He Loves Me, He Loves You Not 2 - Mychea | $14.99 | | |
| He Loves Me, He Loves You Not 3 - Mychea | $14.99 | | |
| He Loves Me, He Loves You Not 4 – Mychea | $14.99 | | |
| Married To Da Streets – Silk White | $14.99 | | |
| My Besties – Asia Hill | $14.99 | | |
| My Boyfriend's Wife - Mychea | $14.99 | | |
| Never Be The Same – Silk White | $14.99 | | |
| Stranded – Silk White | $14.99 | | |
| Slumped – Jason Brent | $14.99 | | |
| Tears of a Hustler - Silk White | $14.99 | | |
| Tears of a Hustler 2 - Silk White | $14.99 | | |
| Tears of a Hustler 3 - Silk White | $14.99 | | |
| Tears of a Hustler 4- Silk White | $14.99 | | |
| Tears of a Hustler 5 – Silk White | $14.99 | | |
| Tears of a Hustler 6 – Silk White | $14.99 | | |
| The Panty Ripper - Reality Way | $14.99 | | |
| The Panty Ripper 3 – Reality Way | $14.99 | | |
| The Teflon Queen – Silk White | $14.99 | | |
| The Teflon Queen 2 – Silk White | $14.99 | | |
| The Teflon Queen 3 – Silk White | $14.99 | | |

| | | | |
|---|---|---|---|
| The Teflon Queen 4 – Silk White | $14.99 | | |
| Time Is Money - Silk White | $14.99 | | |
| Young Goonz – Reality Way | $14.99 | | |
| | | | |
| Subtotal: | | | |
| Tax: | | | |
| Shipping (Free) U.S. Media Mail: | | | |
| Total: | | | |

**Make Checks Payable To:**
**Good2Go Publishing**
**7311 W Glass Lane,**
**Laveen, AZ 85339**

CPSIA information can be obtained
at www.ICGtesting.com
Printed in the USA
LVOW04s1442250116

472165LV00017B/1070/P